# FOLLOW
## THE RIVER

# FOLLOW THE RIVER

## PAUL GRECI

MOVE BOOKS

## ACKNOWLEDGEMENTS:

Many thanks to friends who've gone on wilderness trips with me over the past thirty-five years. All of those experiences have helped shape this story.

Several people had a direct hand in creating this book. Thanks to Sue Dowdell and Micaela Snow for providing thoughtful editorial comments that helped in the development of the story. Many thanks to Illustrator, Jim Madsen, for his masterful artwork. Thank you, Virginia Pope, for designing a beautiful book. Thanks also to Move Books Assistant Julia Sweeney.

Thank you, Eileen Robinson, for the time, energy, and creativity you have invested in my writing.

A big thank you to Amy Tipton, for believing in this story and offering up her editorial expertise in early drafts.

Thank you to my wife, Dana, for being with me on this writing journey every step of the way.

---

## NOTE FROM THE PUBLISHER

*The Move Books team is committed to inspiring readers everywhere.*

---

Library of Congress Control Number:
2021939143

10 9 8 7 6 5 4 3 2 1    21 22 23 24 25 26
Printed in the U.S.A.
First edition, August 2021

74 N. Main Street
Beacon Falls, Connecticut, 06403

To my nephews and nieces:
Jonathan (Oct. 11, 1977 - Oct. 28, 2011),
Mark, Tim, Rebecca, Ruth, Sarah, William,
Hannah, Isabella, Julian, and Anya.
— *Paul Greci*

# CHAPTER 1

**I LIFTED** my paddle one more time, waving to Billy, and then faced forward. I flared my paddle out slightly at the end of every stroke, like Billy had shown me. Otherwise, this rickety old homemade canoe would turn to the opposite side I was paddling on, instead of going straight.

Paddling forward on the right would turn the canoe left.

Paddling forward on the left would turn the canoe right.

I was keeping to the center of the river, trying to dodge the sweepers—those fallen trees still attached by their roots, just lying on the water ready to trap my boat, sink it, and drown me.

The low angle light stretched my shadow thirty or forty feet across the river as I paddled. I glanced over my shoulder again. Billy still stood on the shore, growing smaller by the second. He must have been waiting for me to disappear around a bend before he headed back to the cabin. My arms trembled. A shiver ran up my spine all the way to the top of my head. I wondered if Billy was as nervous and as scared as I was.

I paddled once on the left and once on the right and wondered if I'd ever see Billy again. I wondered if I'd ever see anyone again. Two hundred wilderness river miles separated me from the help I was trying to get for him and his messed-up dad, so I could easily die before reaching my goal. But if I didn't get them help in time . . . I didn't even want to think about it.

Up ahead, the first big bend in the river came into view.

I glanced back one more time. Billy was gone.

The river narrowed.

My heart thumped.

Trees crowded the shore.
I entered the bend.
And that's when I saw it.
A sweeper.

# CHAPTER 2

**I COULDN'T** stay to the inside of the bend because I could see a gravel bar extending into the river, which told me the water was shallow.

The outside of the bend was to my left. And the sweeper hung in the water at the point deepest in the bend.

How would I avoid the sweeper?

How could I keep from running aground?

In a regular canoe it wouldn't be a big deal to scrape the bottom of your boat on a gravel bar. But the shell of my canoe was made of thin, barely-waterproof cloth so scraping bottom could put a big hole in the boat.

The current picked up. I paddled on the left side of the boat, but the way the current ran I was still being pulled to the left—toward the sweeper. So, I switched sides and back-paddled on the right side of the canoe, and that turned me forty-five degrees. Then I paddled forward on the right side but kept flaring my paddle after each stroke.

I could see the bottom on my right, so I did a half-back-paddle on the left side and that got me into deeper water, and I was still far enough away from the sweeper to miss hitting it.

The river straightened out.

Sweat ran into my eyes. I swiped at my forehead. I was happy that I'd remembered Billy's advice about back-paddling, but also realized that paddling solo was going to be a lot of work—both physical work and brainwork.

And I was dead-tired.

From not sleeping more than a couple of hours the past two nights.

From arguing with Billy.

From rescuing Billy and keeping the canoe from sinking.

Mistakes. They happen. But they are more likely to happen when you're so wiped out that you have to concentrate just to keep your eyes open.

But I had to keep going.

I mean, I'd been paddling how long? Maybe only a half hour? I glanced at my wrist ... No watch. I pictured it sitting on the shelf next to my bunk in the one-room cabin. What time was it?

Ten thirty? Eleven o'clock? The sun was still above the treetops but not by much.

As I paddled, I scanned the gear in front of me. At least I had *almost* all the essentials packed in dry bags and tied into the boat—not that it would matter if the canoe flipped, or if I tore a big hole in the bottom, and I drowned.

Tent

Tarp

Sleeping bag

Sleep pad

Cook stove

Cooking pot

Food

Rubber boots

Rain gear

Rope

Bug dope

Clothing

First aid kit

Water bottles

I was missing two important pieces of gear but obsessing about them wouldn't change a thing. I paddled forward. I'd just have to get by with what I had.

A breeze from upriver touched the back of my arms and neck, and I caught a whiff of smoke. Maybe Billy had started a fire in the woodstove at the cabin, and the breeze had blown some of the smoke down here.

The sun was partially blotted out in a cloudy haze now.

My arms shook as I set my paddle across the canoe in front of me, letting the current push me along for a minute. I could feel the water pressing against the bottom of the canoe like the river was going to swallow me whole. I tasted vomit in the back of my throat and turned and spit over the side of the canoe. My twisting motion rocked the canoe. I sucked in a shallow breath and grabbed the paddle as it started to slide.

All I knew about paddling a canoe on a fast-moving river I'd learned from Billy in the twenty minutes we'd spent in the canoe together after I'd rescued him.

The only other time I'd paddled anything had been with my dad in a kayak on the ocean and that had ended in a disaster, which was kind of the reason I was here with Billy, and which was also the reason I was supposed to move to Michigan with my uncle at the end of the summer, which I absolutely didn't want to do.

Then the sun broke out of the haze just above the tree tops and bathed the bank closest to me in a low-angle golden light. It had to be past midnight but this far north the one thing I didn't need to worry about was it getting dark. As tired as I was, I knew I needed to go a little farther before getting some rest.

Just two days ago, me and Billy were getting some distance from Billy's Dad—Mr. Dodge to me—who'd been irate about his own troubles and had basically kicked us out of the cabin for a while. Little did we know that several hours after we'd left the cabin, things would happen that would leave Billy and his dad with injuries so serious they would need help.

# BACK AT THE CABIN
## [TWO DAYS BEFORE THE FIRE]

"Tom," Billy said from behind me as we hoofed it away from the cabin, "my dad has a temper. You know that. Chill out."

"He threw two pieces of firewood at you and was going for another piece," I countered, as I kept the pace brisk. "I've seen him angry but never that angry."

"By the time he meets up with us he'll be calmed down," Billy said. "Trust me."

As I stepped over a downed tree, my foot squished into something soft and made a sucking sound as I pulled it out. I stopped walking and turned to Billy. "Keep an eye out. There's fresh bear scat."

"Nasty." Billy bounced on his toes as he pointed at the mound of scat with my footprint in it. Then he swatted the air to keep the mosquitoes from landing on him.

I tightened my grip around the bear spray. At least we had some protection.

Billy took the lead after we'd encountered the bear scat and set a fast pace—like he was being chased by a forest fire. He's been my best friend since second grade, going on seven years now, and it didn't matter if we were playing video games or shooting arrows, or just talking, Billy was always moving.

We kept walking upriver—I was almost jogging to keep up with him—swatting mosquitoes and bashing through brush. The thorns from the wild rose snagged at my clothes and covered the backs of my hands in scratches, but I'd take the mosquitoes and thorns out in the woods over paddling a flimsy canoe any day. I'd spent the last couple days helping Billy attempt to repair this old homemade canoe, but hadn't told him there was no way I was going to paddle that pile-of-ancient-sticks with him even though he was obsessed with the idea. I'd almost drowned a year ago in a kayak accident and didn't want to place any bets on getting lucky twice.

"Tom." Billy's voice jerked me back into the present. "Look at this."

I ran to catch up. Billy pointed downward. "Tracks. Big dog tracks. Lots of them. Maybe there's someone else out here. There has to be someone with these dogs even though Buck's cabin is the only place up here."

Me, Billy, and his dad had traveled 200 miles by motorboat to get to the cabin. First, 150 miles up the Tanana River and then the last fifty up the Olsen River. The three of us were staying in a cabin owned by *Buck*, one of Mr. Dodge's friends.

Today's plan was for me and Billy to hike about six miles upriver to where the Olsen forks to go fishing and wait for Mr. Dodge there. He was going to replace the prop on the motor and then drive the boat up, and we'd all ride back down to the cabin together. He'd blown his top just before we left and chased us out of the cabin, but Billy was sure he was still going to meet us.

I shouldered in next to Billy and stooped down to study the ground. A mishmash of tracks crisscrossed and lay on top of each other in the mud. "Not dogs." A spot of red stood out on a fallen leaf. I showed it to Billy. "Wolf tracks. And moose, too. They're fresh." Then, I pointed to the ground where drops of blood had hit more leaves. "They must be hunting."

# CHAPTER 3

**AS I** paddled, I thought about the Dodge's. Billy's parents had made it possible for me to stay in Alaska a little longer this summer and spend more time with Billy before I was supposed to move to Michigan with my uncle.

"We'd love to take Tom for a hunk of the summer." Mr. Dodge had said. "I'm taking Billy out to a cabin. We talked it over." He put his arm around Billy. "Tom's welcome to join us. We're hoping to hit the river in about a week."

My Uncle Jim turned to me. "Is this something you want to do? Go up a river and stay in a cabin."

"Yes," I replied. Billy had been talking my ear off about how cool it'd be if his dad could somehow convince my uncle to let me come out to this cabin. And me, I'd do anything to prolong my time in Alaska.

Uncle Jim nodded. "A week should be plenty of time for you to wrap things up around here. We'll have to work out the details of your travel to Michigan."

And now, I'd caused an injury that might kill Billy's dad. And Billy's injury, which I'd also caused, made it even harder for him to take care of his dad. I ground my teeth together.

I had a lot to worry about with keeping this old canoe from going under for two hundred miles of river through empty country, especially since I didn't know much about canoeing.

I needed to keep going but my eyes kept wanting to close, so I reached into the river and splashed some water onto my face.

Stay awake, I thought. Keep paddling. They're counting on you.

Truth was, I was freaked out about camping alone after what had happened the past couple of days.

The longer I stayed in the canoe, the less time I'd have on land. The less time I'd have to worry about being woken by a curious bear. A hungry bear.

Or wolves.

Or a wolverine.

Especially with no bear spray. Nothing to protect myself with, really.

When you're alone, you're alone.

Billy and I had discussed whether I should take the gun, but in the end decided that they should keep it because of what had happened.

The safest place for me was in the canoe, as long as it wasn't sinking.

But I had to rest.

Then my dad's voice popped into my head. He'd been dead for almost a year now, but that didn't stop him from offering up his opinion on all sorts of stuff.

*Tom, find a gravel bar. An island in the river. Stop there. Let the river protect you.*

I remembered lots of islands on the Tanana River but not so many on the Olsen. If I could find a gravel bar attached to land, like the one in front of the cabin, I could camp out in the open and be close to the canoe.

If a bear batted around a metal canoe or a plastic one, it might scratch it or dent it, but if it tangled with my canoe, it could smash it and shred it.

I paddled on the left side of the canoe and moved away from the bank to avoid a sweeper that was still a ways downriver. I was learning to act early to avoid obstacles because the current never stops. It'll push you into anything and everything. The canoe wobbled every time I shifted my weight. It wouldn't take much to tip it.

The sun was below the trees now. My head drooped once, and I sat upright. I needed to find a place to pull out before I fell asleep for real. Plus, all this kneeling was making my legs cramp up, and my ankle, the one I'd broken last year, was tightening up, too.

Up ahead I spotted a tiny spit of land, a narrow gravel bar, jutting out into the river. If I could round it and then pull up behind it, I'd be sheltered from the current and could carefully paddle in. I paddled on the right to move the boat left, and then drifted with the current.

In my head I rehearsed what to do.

Just as I'm passing the spit, I'll back-paddle left. That will point me toward shore. And then I'll paddle forward.

This will be easy, I thought as I maneuvered toward shore.

Boy was I ever wrong.

# CHAPTER 4

**I BACK-PADDLED** and the canoe swung around and pointed toward shore, but in an instant the spit of land I was shooting for was upstream by twenty feet.

I dug my paddle into the water and pulled, but the current kept carrying me farther away from where I wanted to be. I was facing into the current, and the water was streaming around the bow of the canoe like it was a rock in the river.

Get to shore.

Now.

I paddled hard on the left-hand side, trying to angle the boat to the bank, but now the gravel bar was even farther away, and the bank next to me had turned steep, and I was right in the channel where the swiftest water was flowing.

My heart beat a hole through my T-shirt.

Upstream.

Paddle upstream. I kept digging my paddle into the water and flaring it out to keep the canoe pointed where I wanted to go.

I wasn't losing as much ground as I had been when I'd first pointed the boat into the current, but now my gravel bar was forty feet upriver.

I paddled faster, digging my paddle in again and again, wanting to work my way upstream, but because I was also trying to avoid bumping against the cut bank I was steering as much as I was paddling.

And now I started to lose more ground just to keep from bumping into the cut-bank.

Sweat built up on my forehead, and I blinked as a droplet spilled into my eye.

I glanced over my shoulder because I had to see what was behind me. But it was hard to paddle forward and glance backwards at the same time, so I lost a little more ground.

The river was going into a bend, and a blur of dark green hung over the water behind me.

A sweeper.

How close?

I glanced back again and lost a little more ground.

Forward. Focus on the gravel bar. Get there.

Paddle.

Paddle.

Paddle.

Not working, my mind screamed.

Paddle harder.

The sweeper.

I glanced back again.

It was bigger. I was closer. It was closer.

Turn. Turn. Turn.

Get out of here.

Now.

I back-paddled on the left side, and that brought the bow of the boat part way around to the left. I back-paddled again, and the bow swung the rest of the way.

Now I was facing downstream. But doing that back-paddling while facing upriver had moved me downriver quicker than I wanted to be moving right now.

I was still in the main channel.

And the sweeper was almost right in front of me.

And the current wasn't letting up.

Individual needles of the spruce tree hanging in the water came into focus. Little brown cones bobbed in the current. Branches reached underwater.

Branches that could trap anything.

Like a person flailing after his canoe flips.

Like me.

I dug my paddle into the water on the left side of the boat, hoping to get around that sweeper.

Needing to get around that sweeper.

# CHAPTER 5

**THE FRONT** third of the canoe cleared the tip of the sweeper.

I paddled hard on the right side of the canoe, which turned the front of the boat to the left. The tip of the spruce tree connected with the canoe at about its midpoint. Needles made a scratching sound as they ran along the side of the canoe.

The tip of the tree, bobbing in the water, had a little give to it, and the canoe bent it downstream as it rubbed against the end of the sweeper.

And then the canoe floated free, and I was in the current again.

Facing downstream.

I worked my way to the middle of the river. Another bend was coming up, and I wanted to be ready to head left or right to avoid any obstacles.

That's when I caught a taste of smoke and wondered if it was coming from the cabin. The way the river squiggled through the land, smoke blowing in a straight line from the cabin could blow downriver pretty quickly. I wondered how Billy managed to build a fire with his injury and if his dad was even conscious. I hated the fact that at one point me and Billy were almost at each other's throats the day before I set off for help.

"Selfish," Billy had yelled. "I've never seen you act so selfish."

"If selfish means not wanting to die," I shouted back, "then yeah, I'm selfish."

Then before he stormed off, he said, "We're not through with this yet, but right now my dad needs me."

I rounded a mild bend in the river. There were two sweepers on the right side, but I didn't go near enough to them to have to worry, but that also took me out of the main channel, and I discovered that the current slowed way down if you weren't in the channel. I'd have more time to react to obstacles if I weren't in the main channel.

But, it'd take a lot more time and a lot more paddling if I didn't stay in the swift water. And I'd have more of a chance of scraping the bottom in shallow water, which could pepper my canoe with holes.

And there was Billy. And his dad. Especially his dad. Counting on me for help.

But I wasn't some expert canoe-person who could make the boat do what I wanted in an instant.

I caught another whiff of smoke. Maybe some other boaters had come up the Olsen and were camping and I was smelling their campfire. Maybe I wouldn't have to go all the way to where the river first meets up with the highway two hundred miles from here.

I took another breath through my nose and smelled smoke again. I could smell it with every breath now.

"Hello!" I shouted. "Hello." I drifted and listened. I shouted again. I cracked a small smile. I didn't see anyone and no one had yelled back, but if I could survive until tomorrow, I'd probably run into the people whose campfire I was smelling.

A large gravel bar came into view on the right side of the river.

I steered the boat toward the gravel bar. I couldn't let this one get by me.

As much as I wanted to just ram the boat ashore by paddling hard and beaching it solidly, I knew that I could puncture the bottom if I did that.

Beach it gently, I thought. Pull up as close as I can. Hop out and grab the side of the canoe, then ease it onto shore.

I took in another breath with the taste of smoke. I paddled left and the canoe pointed toward shore. I paddled right and the canoe swung back around.

Left.

Right.

Left.

Right.

And now I was twenty feet from the gravel bar, so I paddled my sequence again.

Left. Right. Left. Right.

Five feet from shore I felt a scraping on the bottom. I jumped over the right side of the canoe and held on.

The knee-high river water poured into my rubber boots, but I didn't care. I was holding the boat steady. Easing it into shore.

Now I was in ankle deep water, gripping the side of the boat. I scooted around to the bow and lifted it out of the water and set it down. Then I ran around to the stern and did the same thing. With the canoe completely out of the water, I breathed a sigh of relief.

I could see an orange glow on the horizon, like maybe the sun had swung around and was going to be rising soon. Maybe it was two or three o'clock in the morning. In Alaska in the middle of the summer, this was as dark as it gets. Not even dark enough to need headlights if you were driving.

My eyes were heavy, like weights attached to my eyelids were dragging them down, but I was also starving. I untied the dry bags in the bow of the boat, grabbed the green food bag, opened it, and ate the first thing I found.

A chocolate chip Clif bar.

Then I unclipped my yellow dry bag and dug around until I found a water bottle and took a long drink.

I unloaded the dry bags onto the gravel bar. Then I grabbed the canoe by the side, hoisted it onto my thighs and walked it away from the river to where I could tie it off to a tree in case the river rose while I was sleeping.

I found a flat spot on some small dimension rocks where I could set up the tent.

I hoped there were no bears, wolves, or wolverines close by but didn't have control over that.

After taking the tent, sleeping bag, and sleeping pad from the dry bags, I made a pile of the rest of the bags next to the canoe and put the bag with the cookware on the top, thinking that if anything messed with the bags that one would tumble, and I would hear the pot clanking against the stove in the bag.

And then what would I do?

I eyed the canoe paddle. I'd use it as a club if I had to chase off an animal or protect myself.

I set up the tent and tossed my sleeping pad and bag inside. I took my boots off and wrung my socks out and left them draped over my boots. The bottoms of my pants were wet but were made of thin material. I took my pants off and tried to wring out the bottoms, but there wasn't enough water to make a difference. I tossed my pants in the tent and then climbed in, pulled the paddle in next to me, and zipped the door shut to keep out any mosquitoes that might be on the hunt for some blood. The side of my head hurt a little bit from bumping it on the ground when I'd rescued Billy, but I didn't think it was anything to worry about. I put my hand on the base of the paddle. Could I fight off wolves with it if I needed to?

I lay on my back, closed my eyes, and took a couple of deep breaths. Even inside the tent, I could still smell a little smoke.

# AT THE CABIN
## [TWO DAYS BEFORE THE FIRE]

Wolf and moose tracks crossed our path a bunch of times as we hiked upriver. It seemed like the moose would turn away from the river and then head back, and there was more blood, too. Every time I saw some, I got this weird feeling in my chest, like that moose could be me.

Easily.

Between the bear that had left the fresh scat downriver and the wolves that were most likely chasing a moose upriver, we would have to be on the lookout all the time.

My dad's voice popped into my head.

*It's when you see no signs that you need to pay even closer attention to your surroundings if you want to survive.*

I guess wolves could be close by even if we hadn't seen tracks, and we shouldn't let our guard down. Seeing the tracks and blood is just a reminder that life goes on in the wild the way it's gone on forever.

Eat or be eaten.

I wanted to be one of the ones doing the eating.

"Looks like we'll have to climb the bluff here." Billy pointed ahead. "The bank comes all the way down to the water."

The little strip of flat land we'd been walking on was coming to an end at a big bend in the river. We both peeled our packs off and munched down some crackers and cheese and then gulped water from our water bottles.

"What do you think the wolves did at this spot?" Billy asked.

"Depends on which way the moose went." I slapped a

mosquito caught in the act of making a meal out of my neck. I pointed up toward the bluff. "Maybe there'll be a breeze up there that will keep these blood suckers off of us."

I followed Billy as he worked his way up the hillside. We fought our way through a thicket of wild roses spilling down the slope so we could get into the woods before we'd be cut off and have to swim to keep going upriver.

At the top of the bluff, I grabbed Billy's arm. "You hear that?" I whispered.

Billy opened his eyes wide—like they were about to pop out of his head—and nodded.

Mixed in with splashing sounds were growls, grunts, and high-pitched whimpers, like someone was crying.

"If we go a little further," I whispered, "we should be able to see down into the river."

"Yeah," Billy whispered back. "We need to round the bend."

The *caw* of a raven made my heart jump as the big black bird flapped its wings above us, heading upriver.

The wind was still blowing from upriver, masking our scent from whatever was making all the noise. "Let's keep to the trees," I said. "Hopefully we can see what's happening without being seen." I clicked the safety clip off the bear spray, and now it hung loose on a tiny metal chain just below the trigger. I looked Billy in the eye and said, "Just in case. We need to be ready for anything."

# CHAPTER 6

**I KNEW** I needed to get some sleep but Billy and his dad kept popping into my mind. Not just about Mr. Dodge's injuries but about Mr. Dodge wanting another chance to make things right with Billy. The more I hung around Mr. Dodge, the more I realized that you never knew which Mr. Dodge you would get in any given situation—the nice guy or the mean guy.

My dad had ignored me so much after my mom died that I felt like I'd lost him, too.

When he finally snapped out of his depression after three years, I gave him another chance. But I had a whole history of good times with him to build upon before my mom's death, and from what I knew about Billy and his dad, that was not the case. His dad was often gone for weeks at a time because of his job. And then he'd had a drinking problem that made him act mean. He'd beaten the drinking problem, but it'd taken a long time. And he still had a temper, which he sometimes directed at Billy.

I rolled over in my sleeping bag and lay on my side.

The rainfly on the tent rattled from the breeze, and I smelled smoke again. I moved my ankle around in a circle. It was still tight from all that kneeling in the canoe. And my knees ached, too. If I really wanted to spend all day traveling the river, I'd need to take breaks, which meant I needed to figure out how to land the canoe safely.

An image of that sweeper invaded my thoughts and then I heard my dad's voice.

*Plan far in advance. Be looking downriver for obstacles as far as you can see.*

"I get all that," I said softly. Spotting the obstacles was easy but knowing how to avoid them was the tricky part. The part where, if you made a mistake you could lose your canoe and end up in the water. And if that happened, then what would happen to Mr. Dodge and Billy?

I wished I had the motor boat.

I rolled over to my other side and stretched my legs out.

Sleep on it, I thought. And if I had to I'd only land the canoe in easy spots. And if I needed to stay out of the current because there were too many sweepers in the main channel, then I'd just paddle harder to make up for lost time.

Later, and I didn't know how much later because I didn't have my watch, I woke up. I stretched my arms over my head, and they banged into the door of the tent. I sat up and took a deep breath. Smoke. I still smelled the smoke. Tasted the smoke.

My stomach let out a rumble. I'd known hunger before out on Bear Island. Hunger that could only be solved by hunting, fishing or gathering.

But my food bag in the pile by the canoe would solve my hunger problem, and I'd be able to get on the river with a full stomach. And I'd be able to eat all day long to keep my strength up. Maybe I'd even run into people today so I wouldn't have to worry about drowning or getting eaten by a pack of wolves or a hungry bear.

Maybe I'd find the source of this smoke, someone's campfire or cook fire. I doubted the smell was coming all the way from the cabin.

I unzipped the tent door.

I coughed and I squinted.

And what I saw and felt made my chest go raw on the inside.

# AT THE CABIN
## [TWO DAYS BEFORE THE FIRE]

On the top of the bluff, just back from the edge of the trees, partially camouflaged by low-growing spruce branches and chest-high wild roses, Billy and I stood silently, peering down at the scene playing out in the shallows.

Around the bend the river had widened, and on our side was a shallow, crescent-shaped bay about a hundred feet long. It had grasses growing up through the water, so my guess was that it only filled with water when the river was high.

A mother moose and her long-legged calf stood in the middle of the shallows.

Poking at them from all directions was a pack of wolves.

A jet-black wolf and three gray ones were evenly spread at the edge of the shallows, their muzzles pointing toward the moose like they were spokes on a wheel and the moose was the hub.

The wolves' tails were up and their tips wagging, like if you saw them you would think they were being friendly, not aggressive. The fifth wolf was in deeper water, probably trying to keep the moose from escaping into the river.

The black wolf made a move toward the mother moose, and she charged. Her ears were laid flat on her head as she kicked powerfully with her massive front legs. Big splashes engulfed the black wolf as it retreated to the edge of the water. But this move opened up a shot for one of the gray wolves. It dashed in and nipped at the calf, which let out a high-pitched cry.

*Weeank. Weeank.*

The mother moose turned and charged the gray wolf, and it barely dodged the moose's hooves.

At the same time, the wolf in the deep water worked its way closer to the calf.

The black wolf rushed in. The mother moose splashed and kicked, but this time she trampled her calf and it went down.

One of the gray wolves rushed in and grabbed the calf, but the mother moose charged, and the wolf had to let go and back up to avoid being trampled.

Now all the wolves were standing, not moving.

Billy turned to me and we exchanged a look. His mouth was a round hole between his cheeks, and I'm sure mine was the same.

The wolves didn't seem to be in a hurry. They just kept the pressure on the mother moose—not giving her a way out. The calf was now standing directly under its mother, the mother's legs like protective pillars. The mother moose was moving her head slightly. First in one direction and then back, doing her best to keep track of all four wolves in front of her.

But the wolf behind her, in the deep water, had edged closer, and the mother moose turned her head that way.

When she did this, two of the gray wolves lunged at the mother moose. She lashed out in a fury, creating waves and splashes from forceful kicks as she charged toward them. But this left an opening for the black wolf, which dashed in, grabbed the calf by the face and dragged it toward shore.

I heard Billy suck in a breath like he'd been gut-punched.

# CHAPTER 7

**THE TENT** must've been holding some of the smoke back because the yellow air I stuck my head into instantly made my nostrils itch.

Forest fire.

But where?

How close?

Which direction was it burning?

The small whiffs of smoke I'd tasted yesterday, I realized, weren't from the cabin or someone's campfire.

I put my pants on, crawled all the way out of my sleeping bag, put my damp socks and boots on and stepped out of the tent. In all directions I could see for a couple hundred feet before the smoke made whatever was farther away invisible.

The corners of my eyes itched. I rubbed them, and they itched more.

The year after my mom died had been a record forest fire season in Alaska. There were fires burning in all directions from Fairbanks, so it didn't matter which way the wind was blowing. There was always smoke at our house, and for a few weeks it got as thick as this. Even if you had all the windows closed in your house, it eventually worked its way inside. My dad had a portable air purifier, which he kept running twenty-four hours a day, but it still smelled like smoke inside. I wasn't allowed to play outside because the air was so toxic.

The air was even worse at Billy's house so my dad agreed to have Billy stay with us for a week. We couldn't go outside, so for fun, Billy and I built a fort in the living room out of lightweight wood scraps my dad had left over from various building projects. We never did see flames from our house but I remember my dad checking conditions and making sure he had some supplies packed in his truck in case we had to evacuate.

But this fire? It could be a couple miles away or a couple hundred. The bigger the fire, the more smoke it'd create.

And in these conditions, I realized, no one would be traveling on the river. They'd stay home instead. Mr. Dodge thought I might be able to signal a passing airplane for help if I saw one, but not anymore, not as long as this smoke stuck around.

And, where was the fire? Was it eating up forest and marching my way? What about Billy and his dad at the cabin? They didn't even have a boat to try to escape in. I felt vomit in the back of my throat. I'd never apologized to Billy and he'd never apologized to me, but we had worked out a plan.

I grabbed one of my water bottles and drank it dry. Then I uncapped the other one and took a long drink, but my throat still itched.

Okay, I thought, enough standing around and thinking. You can think as you get ready to go. I set up the stove and filled the pot with water from the river. I needed drinking water and needed to boil it to kill everything so I wouldn't get sick from drinking it. Animals pooped wherever they wanted and their poop had bacteria in it that could cause massive diarrhea if you swallowed it. Beaver fever, some people called it. Always boil your water on the big rivers.

I ate some cheese and crackers, and then when the water was boiling I refilled my two water bottles and left the lids off so the water would cool.

I made some instant oatmeal with the rest of the hot water and scarfed it down straight out of the pot. I wanted a full belly when I hit the river.

The smoke was making my nose run and was still irritating my throat. *You need something between your breath and the smoke. It won't be perfect but it'll help. Something wet, to catch some of the smoke.*

Okay, I thought. Every time I took a drink, my throat felt better, but I couldn't have a shield of water over my nose and mouth. So I worked on the problem as I rinsed the pot at the edge of the river.

A filter. I needed a filter. I remembered wearing a mask to keep from breathing the fumes when I'd helped my dad stain wood for one of his building projects.

It was made of a papery tissue and it covered my nose and mouth. Cloth. I could use cloth.

Back at my pile of gear, I rifled through my clothing bag until I found my bandana. I tied the blue bandana around my face, covering my mouth and nose, like you'd see a bank robber do in an old movie.

*Something wet.*

I jogged to the edge of the river, untied the bandana, soaked it, rung it out, and retied it around my nose and mouth. I took a couple of breaths.

"Okay," I said, like there was someone to talk to. "That's a little better. Not as much of a burn." My eyes still itched, but I couldn't cover them.

I hauled the canoe to the edge of the river, took down the tent and packed all my dry bags and carried them to the canoe. I loaded the canoe and tied the dry bags to the struts, except for the one I was straddling and the one directly in front of me, and then carefully lifted the bow into the water. Next, I raised the stern of the canoe and walked forward until the front two thirds of the canoe were in the river. Then I carefully set the stern down.

I glanced back at my campsite. A faint outline of trees was barely visible through the smoke.

Thanks to my dad, I'd figured out how to breathe less smoke, but now I had another problem to deal with.

Because of the thick smoke, I'd just lost the best thing I had going for me, being able to see things in advance, like sweepers, so I could make a plan to avoid them.

But I had to keep going. Billy and his dad were counting on me even more now. I lifted the stern, set it in the river. The yellow smoke hung downriver like a persistent fog. I wished I knew where the fire was and what direction it was moving.

Was I chasing it or was it chasing me?

# CHAPTER 8
## (BILLY AND HIS DAD)

**"BILLY,"** my dad whispered, "what's that smell? You burn something?"

"Smoke rolled in last night," I replied. "It's pretty thick out there." I thought about Tom being out on the river and wondered how he was dealing with it. "Here, Dad," I nudged his shoulder and then held out a mug with my good hand, "drink some of this."

My dad took the mug of water and sipped, then handed it back to me. "I wish I had a drink. A *real* drink."

"Dad, you beat that," I countered. "Remember what you said? *I can't go down that road again.*"

"That was before," my dad whispered. "Before I thought I might die. Probably will die. I wish I'd brought a bottle." Then he closed his eyes.

"Dad," I raised my voice. "Tom's getting help. You are not going to die. I won't let you." But the truth was, he hadn't moved from his bunk since before Tom left. I'd watched him off-and-on all night long, making sure his chest was rising and falling. I couldn't sleep a wink so I'd paced back and forth in the cabin and just kept checking on him. I didn't know what I'd do if he stopped breathing. I didn't know a thing about first aid.

"This place might burn before help arrives," my dad said softly.

"Tom will come through," I said. "I know he will."

My dad opened his eyes. "Which direction is the fire?"

"I can't tell," I replied. "The smoke is thick everywhere."

He coughed once. "You better figure it out."

# CHAPTER 9

**I TRIED** squinting to keep the smoke out of my eyes as I paddled, but in the end just had to deal with itching and burning.

The river was making a big bend to the left. I didn't want to get carried to the outside of the bend, so I paddled on the left and that moved the canoe to the right.

In the middle, I thought, stay in the middle of the river, even though the current would move me faster if I steered into the outside of the bend. But that's also where the cut banks and sweepers were more common. At least that's what I thought from what I'd seen yesterday.

I was learning with every paddle-stroke. The more I paid attention to how the boat responded, the more likely I could make the right decisions when faced with sudden obstacles. The more likely I wouldn't wrap the canoe around a rock or snag it on a sweeper.

As I rounded the bend, a breeze pressed my bandana-mask onto my face. It wasn't super strong, but it was brisk enough that I felt the resistance as I paddled. On the left side of the river, through the smoke, I spotted a sweeper. A fat spruce tree jutting about fifty feet into the river.

The tip of the tree bobbed in the water.

On shore I heard a rustling noise.

I peered through the smoke.

The wind was blowing through the tops of the trees, causing the leaves on the aspens and birches to shake. At river-level the wind didn't seem as strong but I could still feel it slowing me down.

And then I heard a breathing noise.

It was more of a whisper, but it was steady and rapid, like every second a small breath was being sucked in.

I set my paddle down and rubbed my burning eyes and kept listening. The noise grew louder, even though it was still incredibly soft, like whatever was making it was now closer to the canoe.

What swims in a river?

Beavers.

Otters.

But with all the otters and beavers I'd seen, I'd never heard any of them breathing like this. They moved quietly in the water. Otters were hunters. And beavers, the only time I'd heard them make noise in the water was when they'd slap their tails.

Breath.

Breath.

Breath.

And then I saw it. A tiny head. Really just half-a-head. Its nose and eyes above the water and its jaw and mouth below. Its little legs must've been working like crazy, made more for climbing trees than swimming.

I turned and looked over my shoulder as it passed behind the canoe. It must've come from the right shore because it was heading to the left and it was way out here in the middle. The breathing noise grew faint as I continued to drift down river and the squirrel continued to cross.

I'd never seen a squirrel swim. I'd never even heard of squirrels swimming.

I couldn't imagine that the spruce cones were so much better on one side of the river than the other. And even if they were, would a squirrel knowing that?

Something must've really scared it to chance a swim across the river. But usually squirrels ran up trees when they got scared or startled. That's what they were made to do. And, there were plenty of trees on both sides of the river.

I set my paddle in the boat, grabbed my water bottle, lifted my bandana and took a drink. Then I reached over the side of the canoe, cupped my hand and splashed water into my eyes to try to ease the itching.

A swimming squirrel, I thought. My dad would've loved to see that tiny tree-climber crossing a big river. He'd put a lot of energy into squirrel-proofing our bird-feeder.

*But what does it mean?*

I picked up my paddle and dug the blade into the water, pouring over my dad's question. Did it really have a meaning?

*Everything has a meaning whether you see it or not.*

Then it hit me.

There was only one thing that would cause a squirrel to cross a wide, fast-moving river. One thing that a squirrel couldn't escape by climbing a tree.

And that one thing it had to be escaping?

Fire.

I sucked in a breath.

The cabin was on the right side of the river—the same side the squirrel had come from.

# CHAPTER 10

**HOW WERE** Billy and Mr. Dodge reacting to being stranded in all this smoke? What were they doing? What could they do besides wait? What had happened to Mr. Dodge's leg had been bad enough but my actions—my one action—had made things a hundred times worse.

After the disaster on Bear Island, the Dodges took me in. Eventually my uncle got involved but the Dodges were the closest thing to family I had. They understood what I'd been through.

For the first few weeks living with them, Billy talked a mile a minute but all I could do was muster up one and two word responses.

"Give Tom time," I overheard Mrs. Dodge saying to Billy. "He needs to re-integrate."

"What's that mean?" Billy asked.

"He has to adjust to being around people again," Mrs. Dodge responded. "He's been alone for a long time."

"He'll be okay," Mr. Dodge added. "We won't let him out of our sight until he is."

I doubled down on my paddling.

But fires can travel fast. A couple years ago a whole fire crew, like seventeen people, died fighting a fire. And they were experts, following orders.

My head hurt. It was like the smoke had irritated my eyes and the irritation had clawed its way inward.

The smoke was so thick that you couldn't even see an outline of the sun.

I rounded another bend and the wind picked up, causing little ripples to form on the river and move in the opposite direction of the current.

The headwind slowed me down. I broke a sweat as I continued to dig the old wooden paddle into the disturbed water, flaring it out after every stroke in an attempt to keep the boat pointed in the direction I wanted to go. But the bow would catch the wind and swing out, and I'd be pointed toward shore. If only I had Billy in the front of the boat paddling with whatever homemade paddle he'd planned on making. We'd be going twice as fast, maybe faster.

But those thoughts did me no good because Billy wasn't going to magically show up. Even if he did, he only had one good arm because of what had happened.

*Keep thinking.*

"Yeah, right," I said.

*Keep going with Billy. What else did he do? What doesn't happen when he's not in the boat?*

Now, I'd heard my dad's voice enough times to know that most of the time when it tried to tell me something or show me something, it didn't come right out and say the answer or the solution like I wished it would. Usually it just gave hints, pointing me in the direction he wanted my thinking to take.

Billy in the boat, I thought. For the few minutes we had been in the canoe together, he'd kept watch for rocks and logs. He held the canoe onshore while I got out of it. Big deal. I was watching for rocks as best I could from the stern, and I'd figured out how to get the boat close enough to shore to hop out and guide it in without scraping up the bottom too badly.

Billy in the boat.

Boat.

Billy.

Boat.

Billy.

I pictured him sitting up front.

A big gust of wind slammed me from the side and turned the canoe ninety degrees so it was pointing toward shore. I back-paddled and got it pointed downriver again. Through the smoke I saw a sweeper on the left side, so I steered the boat to the right.

Another gust of wind tried to swing the bow sideways, but I back-paddled and kept it pointed downriver. But all this back-paddling was slowing my progress.

I uncapped my water bottle and drank what was left in it. And suddenly I was hungry. And my legs and knees and ankle were rebelling against all this kneeling.

Up ahead I spotted a sandy beach. A nice place to land, I thought. A place to dig some food out of a dry bag and get my other water bottle out. And a place to stretch my legs.

I angled the canoe toward shore. One thing about me being in the boat alone was that I could approach shore really closely before being in danger of hitting the bottom. With Billy in the boat we'd bottomed out a lot sooner because of all the weight in the front of the canoe.

The weight.

His weight, I thought.

That's what's different.

But why would it matter?

Another gust of wind blew the bow around, and I back-paddled to counter it.

And then I had it. I knew what Billy provided for the canoe when he was here. Now I just needed to figure out how to replicate it.

# CHAPTER 11

**ON SHORE,** I unpacked the bow of the canoe. I opened the green dry bag with the food and inhaled a couple of chewy chocolate chip granola bars. When I lifted the bandana so to eat, I discovered that it had dried out, so after I ate I drenched the bandana in river water, wrung it out and retied it.

The smoke was still burning my eyes and my head still hurt, but there wasn't much I could do about those two things so I set about doing something I could change.

It was sandy where I'd landed the boat, but just down the shore it got rocky and it was rocks I was looking for. Medium-sized, smooth, rounded rocks.

Once I figured out what my dad had meant, I didn't know why it'd taken me so long. He'd said the same thing about me when I was sitting in the front seat of the kayak and he was in the back. He'd called me *ballast*.

I remembered a ballast is weight used to stabilize a boat. If I could get the bow of the canoe to sit a little lower in the water, then it wouldn't be blown around as much by the wind. I didn't have an extra dry bag to fill with sand or gravel or small rocks, so I was looking for a few bigger rocks that I could just put on the floor of the canoe right in the tip of the bow. Then I could put my gear over them and be on my way, hopefully with a canoe that wouldn't get so blown around.

I found three rounded rocks. Each was about twice the size and more elongated than a large grapefruit. I'm not sure how much they weighed, but I could only carry one at a time.

I lifted the bow of the canoe and set it in the water. Then I nestled the three rocks as close to the tip of the bow as I could get them. That made the front of the canoe touch the river bottom, so I lifted it and eased it farther out until it floated free.

And all this time I realized, no mosquitoes had harassed me.

Maybe the smoke was keeping them from being active because right this minute the wind wasn't blowing onshore, which is the only other thing that would keep the bugs from swarming me.

I ate some peanuts and drank some water and then loaded the dry bags on top of the rocks and tied them in. The rest of the canoe was already packed except for the medium-sized yellow dry bag that was usually clipped to the strut right in front of me. I put my empty water bottle inside it. The other bottle was about three quarters full. That would have to do me for the rest of the day because I didn't want to stop to boil water until I was stopping for the night, and I still had hours to go before that would happen.

I decided to keep that bottle loose in the boat so I could drink. I stuffed a Clif Bar into my back pants pocket so I could eat without having to unclip the bag.

After clipping the yellow bag in, I splashed water on my eyes and on the bandana covering my face. I wished I had some sunglasses too, but they'd disappeared in the mess we'd found at the cabin when we finally made it back from our hike upriver. I did a final check on the sandy beach to make sure I didn't leave anything behind.

Then, just above the treetops where the beach turned to forest, I spotted them. At first, I thought, snow. It couldn't be snow, but that's what my mind did when it saw the white flakes drifting down.

Ash.

Ash. Ash. Ash.

And that made me think about the fire and how close it might be. I wasn't just paddling through smoke, because the smoke was a result of the fire. Or fires. And I still didn't know how close or how far away or in what direction an actual fire might be.

I glanced upriver wondering if it was raining ash on the cabin too.

I caught one piece of ash on my fingers and rubbed it, and it disintegrated.

I pictured the container with my mom's ashes back at what used to be my house in Fairbanks. I would be taking those with me to Michigan, but really, they belonged in Alaska. And that bothered me. I belonged in Alaska and that bothered me, too. I needed to figure out a way to stay. A way to be true to myself and what I wanted and needed.

I was so angry with my uncle. I'd been staying with Billy's family for months and then he'd come out of nowhere and taken over my life.

"I've accepted an offer on the house and the land," Uncle Jim had said as we both stood in the living room.

I thought about all the time I'd spent with my mom and dad on this land. We owned forty acres, and my dad had made trails so we could really explore. "Why can't you just rent it out until I'm eighteen, and then I'll come back and take care of it?" I'd asked.

"Your dad owed a lot of money on this place, and then the mortgage went unpaid for months after you two went missing. And, he'd run his savings way down since your mother died." My uncle took a breath. "At least I got the bank to withhold any penalties but paying the last several months' mortgage has me stretched pretty thin."

"What about me?" I raised my voice. "This is my home. It's all I've got, and I don't want to sell it." My dad had fixed up this house with his own two hands. He'd knocked walls down to open up the living space and he'd installed more windows so the south-facing wall was mostly glass. How could my uncle even think of selling it?

"We need to sell. The money will be put into an account, and you'll get that when you turn eighteen unless I feel you need to mature more before taking on the responsibility of managing money."

"Whatever," I said. "I'll just buy it back when I turn eighteen."

"That's unlikely," my uncle countered. "When we sell, we have to pay what we owe on the mortgage. What you'll get is what is left after that. It won't be enough money to buy the place back." My uncle took a step toward me. "That's just the way it is," he said softly. "I'm sorry."

"I can't just leave everything," I said. "I just got back."

"There's two big boxes," my uncle said, pointing, "anything you can fit into them, I'll mail to Michigan. Pack them up before you leave for the cabin with Billy and Mr. Dodge. And, if you've got anything big you want to take, like your mom's guitar, or your dad's folding kayak, just set it with the boxes and I'll take care of it."

But right now, I couldn't deal with any of that.

I lifted the stern of the canoe and walked forward, pushing the canoe into the river. When it floated free, I jumped in, knelt on the knee pads I'd made at the cabin to protect my knees from the knobby wood of the bottom frame of the canoe, and started paddling.

If there are ashes here, then the fire can't be far away.

Then that swimming squirrel popped back into my mind, and I knew that at least one fire had to be close by. I fished my ball cap out of the dry yellow bag, hoping it'd help keep ash from getting into my eyes.

Then I dipped my paddle into the river and pulled, realizing I could be paddling away from one fire and into another.

# AT THE CABIN

## [TWO DAYS BEFORE THE FIRE]

The moose calf let out a whimper, and the mother moose advanced on the black wolf, but then she stumbled, like maybe one of her front legs sunk into the mud, and instantly the other four wolves were on her. One grabbed her by the nose and another by the neck, and the other two latched onto her spine, avoiding her back legs that were kicking.

The moose fell farther onto her side, and the wolves kept her head in the water in the shallows. Her back legs kept kicking, but the wolves on her spine were still out of range, pulling and tugging with their entire bodies, so the moose's kicks touched only air. The wolves on her neck and nose kept driving downward to keep her head under water. Her legs kept moving but the power in her kicks was fading.

Minutes went by as me and Billy watched in silence from the bluff-top.

The two wolves who were attacking her spine had moved to her front and now we could see guts spilling out of her from the wounds they had opened up.

At the same time the black wolf had dragged the calf all the way out of the water and was eating it alive. Every so often you could see movement from one of the calf's legs, but eventually it lay still.

My eyes kept bouncing between the killing scenes.

The four wolves worked at dragging the mother moose to the edge of the water until her back was barely in the shallows. Then they all concentrated on her midsection. And still her legs kept kicking weakly for a minute or two longer and then went still.

Now their tails were mostly down as they tugged on the moose and tore off pieces of meat. When the gray wolves looked up, we could see their faces, covered in pink from the blood.

The black wolf continued to work on the calf alone, ripping pink hunks of flesh and gulping them down, doing almost no chewing, just swallowing.

At intervals, each wolf stopped eating in order to drink some water from the river.

And during all this time, more and more ravens gathered. Some perched in trees and others circled overhead, cawing. And a few bold ones landed on the ground close to the wolves.

Killing.

It was messy.

But that was part of survival.

I thought about Mr. Dodge, who was supposed to be motoring upriver to meet us at the forks. With the wolves right in front of us, combined with the bear scat we'd seen, I didn't want to miss him. The wolves would probably scatter if he came motoring up now. If he did scare the wolves, I hoped they wouldn't all come running in our direction.

I glanced down at the bear spray in my hand. It would probably work on one wolf but I doubted there was enough spray to turn back five of them.

# CHAPTER 12

## THE ROCKS

I put in the bow made the boat ride a little lower in the water so when the wind gusted it didn't blow it around as much.

The ash kept raining down. It coated everything in the boat just like snow would do, which made me think of the one major snowstorm we had last winter.

It was late February and I'd been living with the Dodge's for almost three months. I was still using crutches for my ankle but it was snowing about an inch an hour and Billy was dying to get out in it but he really wanted me with to go with him.

"If Tom slips and falls," Mrs. Dodge said, "it'll set him back," putting a stop to Billy's idea that we take a short walk to check out the storm.

You just go, Billy," I said. "I'll be fine right here."

Billy shook his head. "No deal. If you stay in, I stay in." Billy raised his eyebrows. "But...." He put a finger in the air. "Mom, you said Tom can't *walk* in the storm, right?"

Mrs. Dodge put her hands on her hips. "That's right. I—"

But Billy was out the door and into the garage before she could finish. In a flash he was back in the kitchen holding a six-foot-long plastic sled. "Tom won't have to walk." He turned to me. "I'm pulling you and I won't take *no* for an answer."

Now, as I rounded a bend saw a slew of heads swimming about one hundred feet in front of the canoe, crossing the river from right to left. They crawled out of the water, and on the bank, I counted four fox—one big one and three little ones—shaking river water off themselves like dogs as the ash continued to fall.

I wondered what they made of me as I drifted by. They didn't seem to be in a hurry to disappear into the forest. They just watched, their heads tracking my movement.

And then I wondered if animals sometimes called a truce when bigger things, like surviving a fire, were affecting them. Like if that squirrel swimming across the river had hauled out near the fox, would they just let it be for now, thinking, *yeah, you're just getting out of the way of the fire, too.*

Fire or no fire, the fox still had to eat. But still, I wondered. Out on Bear Island, sometimes bears tried to take my food and sometimes they didn't. Maybe whether the fox tried to chase down and kill a squirrel just depended on how hungry they were.

The fox family disappeared into the forest and I kept paddling. I rounded the next bend and was hit by a gust of wind head on. I could control the boat better with the rocks in the bow, but it was still a major pain to paddle solo into a headwind.

The strong gusts kept coming, blowing the ash under the rim of my cap. I squinted, trying to keep it out of my eyes, but they began to itch way more than when it had been just smoke irritating them. I reached one hand over the side of the canoe, cupped some water and splashed it into my eyes, and that helped a little but they still itched, especially right in the corners.

The river was making a long bend to the right, and the shore changed abruptly to fifty-foot tall bluffs on the right side. The land leading down to the river wasn't sheer, but you couldn't climb up it without a rope. Plants grew in pockets. I spotted wild rose blooming and fireweed that was tall and green and hadn't yet bloomed. Through the yellow smoke I studied the top of the bluff.

And it was up there that I caught my first view of yellow-orange as a spruce tree burst into flames.

# AT THE CABIN

## [TWO DAYS BEFORE THE FIRE]

"It's like this," Billy whispered. "My dad loves moose meat. After the wolves leave, if there's any leftover, we should cut off a hunk." Billy patted his pocket. "I've got my knife."

I turned away from the wolves and faced Billy. "So, we just walk down there and carve a hunk a meat out of the carcass?" I shook my head. "Wolf slobber all over it? Sick."

"Tom," Billy responded, "You told me you ate salmon that a bear had killed. I don't—"

"That was to keep from starving," I interrupted. "It was gross but I didn't have a choice."

One of the wolves let out a sharp bark, and Billy and I turned and looked. Now they were all staring upriver. They stayed that way for about a minute and then went back to eating.

Billy tapped my shoulder and whispered, "My dad would be proud. We'd actually get to give him something."

I didn't want to let Billy down. I was already planning on backing out of canoeing with him. Plus, I knew he'd had some tough times with his dad. I remembered when Billy came to school in fourth grade with a bruised arm—it was a few months after my mom had died—and had told me, his dad had done it, but said it was an *accident*. And when I pressed him on it, he finally told me that his dad had hit him with a shovel but made me promise I'd never tell anyone.

"You're sure you want to give your dad a piece of moose meat with wolf slobber all over it?" I asked.

Billy smirked. "You used to pick marshmallows up out of the dirt and eat them. Remember?"

"I was little then," I reasoned. "I didn't care. But wolf slobber? That's just sick."

"We'll cook the meat and it'll kill all the germs." Billy pointed to me. "You ate bear slobber and you're still alive."

"I think it's kind of risky to approach a carcass."

"We won't go down there until we're sure the wolves are gone," Billy countered. "There's no way those wolves will eat every last bit of that moose. We'll get a piece and then head to the forks. Maybe it'll help snap my dad out of his mood."

I sighed, then nodded. "I'll stand guard with the bear spray while you cut into the moose."

I had a bad feeling about this. I hoped Mr. Dodge would come motoring up before we put this plan into action.

# CHAPTER 13

**I WATCHED** in sick fascination as the fire ate the tree. Then I noticed, through the thick smoke, more flames traveling through the underbrush where the bluff sloped downward and allowed me a view. A red-lava glow silhouetted the burnt-to-black remains of spruce trees.

As I got deeper into the bend, I could see more trees actively burning. It appeared to be traveling upriver on the right side. The spruce trees were bursting into flames while the birches were getting charred but not totally burning up.

Sparks were flying, being carried up through the smoke. A hot wind pressed on me from the fire, so I steered the boat more toward the center of the river. The bluff was coming to an end, and the fire was burning on the low banks that replaced it. Flames crackled, like someone had cranked up the volume on a huge bonfire.

At Billy's house there was a woodstove with a glass door so you could see the flames and when they first took me in, I basically lived by that fire, just watching the flames.

"You sure do like sitting by that fire," Mr. Dodge had said, taking a seat next to me.

"On Bear Island," I responded, "fire was the only friend I had."

Mr. Dodge put his hand on my shoulder. "You've got us now. I know we can't take the place of your dad, but we're here for you."

"Thanks," I said. I knew Mr. Dodge had an anger problem but he also had a kind side to him.

I flared my paddle and worked my way to the left side of the river, wanting to get as far away from the fire as possible. A burning spruce that was leaning out over the river on the right bank fell into the water and made a splash. Steam rose from the spot where the newly created charred sweeper bobbed in the current, just barely hanging onto the bank with its roots.

Up ahead on the left, a moose cow and calf, soaking wet, stood on a gravel bar. They must've just swum across.

Then I passed a whole patch of spruce forest on the right that hadn't burned, but just downriver more forest was burning.

What determined where the fire burned?

Wouldn't the whole forest burn up until it rained really hard or firefighters had put out the fire? Would firefighters even fight a fire way out here?

And then I realized that I had a lot to learn about wildfires and that I better learn it soon because I was traveling through one.

*Stay in the river.*

"Right," I said. Even though I was basically in an oven, a shiver ran through my body and made me itchy, like the only way to get relief would be to crawl out of my own skin.

Water.

It was the only thing that could save me but it still might not be enough. I could still be burned alive.

I studied the far side of the river, seeing charred areas that were still burning and other spots that were green.

There's a chance, I thought, that the fire would burn through the woods around the cabin.

But there's a chance it wouldn't.

The cabin had a metal roof. That might help keep it safe. My stomach clenched up. They couldn't even run. They could be burned alive too.

I heard a cracking, splitting sound, and through the smoke spied one flaming tree falling into another.

Then a gust of wind lifted my hat, and I caught it just before it would have been air-born.

This action caused me to look straight up and that's when I saw them.

Little red embers being blown through the sky across the river, every one of them a potential fire-starter.

# AT THE CABIN

## (TWO DAYS BEFORE THE FIRE)

By the time the wolves left the kill, Mr. Dodge still hadn't appeared with the motor boat and now Billy was itching to get a piece of moose meat for his dad.

"The wolves are long gone." Billy said. "Let's do this."

The ravens that had been waiting like we had now blanketed the carcass.

I pointed at the big black birds. "There's at least forty ravens chowing down right now. You sure you want to give your dad a piece of moose that birds have been pecking on? Don't they carry diseases?"

Billy bounced on his toes. "I'll tell my dad about the birds and let him decide if he actually wants to eat it. I just want to give it to him."

Even though I knew approaching a carcass wasn't the smartest thing to do, I didn't want to get in the way of Billy doing something for his dad. If my dad were still alive and I could do something to make him proud or happy or impressed, even if it involved some risk, I'd do it, too.

I looked Billy in the eye. "Okay," I said. "Let's get this over with." I grabbed my backpack, put it on, and then picked up the bear spray.

"Now you're talking." Billy tapped me on the shoulder, cracked a smile, and then pointed toward the carcass. "Moose meat doesn't get much fresher than that."

Me and Billy worked our way down from the bluff. The ravens were a noisy bunch focused on filling up on moose meat.

I wondered what they'd do when we approached the carcass.

I rubbed the scar under my ear.

Ever since being attacked by a swan on Bear Island, I didn't just assume birds would fly away when approached.

Hopefully they wouldn't attack in mass.

We kept angling our way down since the bluff was so steep and ended up a couple hundred feet upriver from the carcass.

We picked our way along the shore. I had the safety clip on the bear spray. I hoped the wolves wouldn't show back up and wondered if the spray would work on them. Then I thought about bears. This carcass would definitely attract bears.

I stopped walking. With my thumb, I popped the safety clip off the trigger on the bear spray, and it now dangled from a small chain.

Billy, who was beside me and had stopped when I stopped, glanced at the canister in my hand. "Expecting company?"

I took a breath and looked around. "It's a carcass with a loud bunch of ravens on it. Every meat-eater who has half-an-ear is going to come running, just like we did."

# CHAPTER 14

**A GRAY**-black column of smoke was rising from the bluff-top behind me. And the thick yellow air I'd been breathing was still here, too. Like the old smoke was settling while the new smoke from the active part of the fire was rising.

And one more thing I noticed about the air.

It was still getting warmer.

The wind was pushing the fire from right to left, and even on the left side of the river I could feel the heat.

I looked up and saw more red embers mixing with the ash in the sky. I didn't see any fire on the left side of the river, but all it would take was one ember because the forest was so dry.

I kept paddling, trying to hug the left bank, but the river was bending right and there was a series of sweepers poking out from the left bank so I steered to the middle of the river to avoid them. And in just that short distance I felt the heat increase. Sweat broke out on the right side of my face.

Fingers of fire had burned all the way down to the riverbank, but areas of green remained too. And I noticed that there were mostly birch trees in the unburned areas.

My mind kept working on the river. I needed to reach the Tanana River as soon as I could. It was massive compared to the Olsen. Like if the fire was on one side, there would be less of a chance that it could jump the river. And, if I could stay in the middle of a big river I'd probably be safe if the fire was raging on both sides. But if the fire was raging on both sides of the Olsen....

*Stay in the river.*

"Yeah," I said. "I heard you the first time."

Could I paddle all day and all night? I didn't know if I could stay awake. And it wasn't just a matter of staying awake. I had to be alert, too.

I flared my paddle and steered back toward the left side of the river now that I was around the bend and the sweepers were behind me.

The fire raged in a patch of black spruce on the right side. It popped and crackled as a swirl of black smoke rose through the yellow sky. So I splashed more water on my bandana, took my hat off, dipped it in the water, and then put it back on.

A light layer of ash now covered my dry bags inside the canoe, but I didn't care as long as no red embers landed in my boat. And, as long as I could keep far enough away from the fire to keep from being burned alive. I wished I could transport myself out of this mess. I wished I had someone to help me. My chest tightened up. I took some deep breaths but instead of helping, they just made me cough.

"Keep it calm," I said to myself. "Keep it calm. You make a mistake now and you could be stuck in a fire. Then you could get burned alive. Right now, you're on the river. Okay? I told myself. Okay." But it wasn't okay. I was scared out of my mind but I couldn't let panic take over, then I'd make a mistake for sure.

The river grew narrower, snaked left, and then right. I paddled hard, looking for rocks or logs to avoid but didn't see any.

Then it widened again. But the wind picked up, driving ash and embers crosswise. Little black coals—burnt up pieces of trees—bobbed in the current. A red ember landed on the yellow dry bag in front of me so I reached into the river and splashed water on it before it could cause any damage. The bottom of the boat had gray padding beneath the knobby wood frame and on top of the thin white fabric so if an ember landed on the floor of the canoe at least it wouldn't land directly on the thin, white, fabric.

Another ember landed in the canoe and started to melt the gray padding so I splashed water on it. I grabbed the cold ember and chucked it into the river. One or two embers at a time I could handle but what if an army of embers parachuted in? Then what would I do? My canoe was made of fabric and wood. If I got overwhelmed by embers, it would burn.

Easily.

Too easily.

On the right, the bank built itself into a high bluff, at least a hundred feet above the river. Up there I could see blackened, recently burned spruce trees bending toward the river in the stiff breeze.

And on the left side of the river I saw smoke.

And flames.

Jumped, I thought. The fire had already jumped the river.

And I was in the middle.

I wondered how hot the ground was in the recently burned areas. Like if I had to beach the canoe and walk, could I walk through recently burned forest or would my rubber boots melt?

I was on this narrow strip of water, threading my way through a fire in a boat that was built to burn. I dug my paddle in and pulled. I had to reach the wide expanse of the Tanana, but I also had to rest at some point because if I fell asleep while paddling, I could drift right into the fire.

I grabbed my water bottle, lifted my bandana off my mouth and took a drink. The bottle was only a quarter full.

Should I drink the river water without boiling it? The thought of getting diarrhea wasn't a welcome one. If I could find a safe place to rest and stretch my legs, I could light the stove, boil some water, eat a bunch of food and then keep paddling.

There were pockets of green, unburned vegetation on both sides of the river, but often the fire was burning right up to the edge of them and I didn't want any part of that.

"Okay," I said. "I'll only stop if it looks safe. And if I do stop, it will be for a very short time." And if I can't stop, I thought, I'll just drink river water and deal with the diarrhea if I get it. I kept on paddling, closing my brain down to concentrate on covering some distance. I got into a rhythm.

Three paddle strokes on the right.

Three paddle strokes on the left.

And I just kept doing that. And every time my paddle hit the water, I said the word *paddle* out loud so my mind didn't have time to obsess over anything that I couldn't change, or anything that I wished were different, which was pretty much everything starting from about four years ago onward—when my mom had died.

I don't know how long I paddled like that. My arms were turning to rubber. The fire still burned on both sides of the river, but then I came around a bend and saw a potential place to take a break and boil some water. It was just downriver a couple hundred yards. My knees were screaming for relief louder than my arms, my water bottle was long empty, and the Clif bar in my back pocket was a memory.

I dug my paddle in, steering for the spot, not realizing until after I pulled up and jumped out of the canoe that I had company.

# AT THE CABIN

## [TWO DAYS BEFORE THE FIRE]

We were ten feet from the carcass. The off-white from the ends of some of the rib-bones where the meat had been almost completely torn off stood out from the black of raven feathers.

The big birds continued to peck and squawk. One flew off with a piece of moose guts dangling from its beak and another chased it.

I took two steps forward and waved my arms. "Skedaddle," I shouted. Then I took another step and did it again, and the whole flock of ravens lifted off in protest, leaving me and Billy with what was left of the wolf-killed moose.

"Last fall, I helped my dad butcher the one and only moose he ever got," Billy said, studying the mess in front of us. He pointed at the hind end of the moose. "I think there's a hunk of untouched meat just up from where that leg used to be attached."

"Just cut a piece and let's get out of here," I said.

"Tom, just chill out." Billy bounced on his toes. "This is supposed to be fun. Don't wreck it."

I swallowed once. "Whatever. Just do it." Maybe Billy was right. Maybe I was making a bigger deal out of this than I needed to. "Sorry," I said, and attempted a smile.

Billy grinned back at me and then fished a small knife out of his pocket and pulled it open. "I thought the knife would come in handy if we caught a fish. But a moose?" He laughed.

At least he was still in a good mood. He had enough to deal with given his dad's anger problem. If a piece of moose meat would pacify Mr. Dodge, I was all for it. Still, I didn't like hanging out next to a carcass.

The ravens were in the trees above us, cawing up a storm and making it hard to hear, so I was glancing all around, looking for any movement I might have to deal with.

Billy knelt on the ground with the small pack on his back, and the knife in his hand. "Okay," he said, "here goes."

Billy started carving a hunk of meat out of the carcass. While he worked away, I was turning slow small circles, studying the woods and brush in all directions.

After a minute or so, I saw movement in the brush upriver right where Billy and I had come down off the bluff.

Then my heart shot up my throat and lodged itself on to the roof of my mouth as a snarling wall of fur rushed toward us.

# CHAPTER 15

## (BILLY AND HIS DAD)

**MY DAD** closed his eyes and whispered, "I promised your mother I'd get you home safely. Looks like it's going to be up to you to keep that promise."

"I know you're splitting up," I said.

My dad cracked his eyes open. "Your mother," he paused, "and you, put up with a lot from me. You're stuck with me as your father, but your mother, she's done. I don't blame her." He squeezed his eyes closed and then opened them again. "I blame me."

This was the first time I had ever heard my dad take blame for anything. "Maybe you and mom can still work it out."

"I'm sorry," he whispered, "for every time I've laid a hand on you. I don't expect you to forgive me." He paused. "I just want you to know I'm trying to change."

I thought back to a couple of days ago when he was throwing firewood at me. He might never change but here he was saying he was trying.

I paced back and forth across the cabin floor, and then stopped at his bedside. "I'll give you a chance."

"If you see flames," he said, "get yourself into the river. Don't die trying to save me." He closed his eyes. "I can't even get out of this bunk, let alone walk. Save yourself."

"We just have to make it until Tom gets us some help," I said.

He shook his head. "If this place goes up in flames, leave me. End of discussion."

I walked across the cabin and peered out the window next to the door. It was like trying to see through mustard. I glanced back at my dad. No way would I let him die out here. Not if I could help it.

# CHAPTER 16

**I WASN'T** exactly in the middle of the river, but I was close. I'd beached the canoe on the upstream side of a small, narrow island about a hundred feet long and thirty feet wide at its widest point—the first island I'd seen since leaving the cabin.

The bottom end of the island had a clump of trees, but the top end, where I'd landed, was bare except for some scraggly shin-high patches of not-yet-bloomed fireweed.

That little group of trees at the bottom end of the island was why I hadn't seen the company until after I'd landed. And once I stood up and stretched my knees, no way did I want to hop right back in that canoe—unless I was going to get charged or stomped, which were both possibilities.

I kept my eye on the four moose as I stood on shore and gripped the side of the canoe to keep it from floating away.

The two mother moose were potentially dangerous, but their calves were not.

And, maybe there were more that were still hidden in the trees.

On shore, the fire was burning pretty strong. Black Spruce were lighting up, the brush under them was flaming, but the birch trees seemed to be doing okay. Their trunks were charred and some leaves had dried and burnt, but they weren't bursting into flames like the spruce. And, no embers had ignited the forest on the island—yet.

On the far side of the river, I could see fire both above and below the spot directly across from the island, which made me think that the embers were jumping over in lots of places.

But back to the moose. The adult moose were big enough to stomp me flat and destroy my canoe. And I'm sure they'd do that if they thought I was threatening their calves. Each calf stuck close to an adult.

Two mother-baby pairs, I thought.

Moose Nursery Island, I'd call it.

I wasn't planning on exploring the island. I was content to hover in my tiny spot, boil up some water, wolf down some food and then shove off.

The mother moose were both looking in my direction. Instead of looking right back at them, I decided to just go about my business and watch them out of the corner of my eye.

The wind was whipping through the narrow channel between the island and the shore, carrying a continuous slug of warm air. I scooted down to the bow of the canoe, turned my back to the moose, and carefully lifted the boat. I set it down so half of the bow was onshore and half was in the shallows so it wouldn't swing out into the current. Keeping my hands on the side of the canoe, I walked to the stern and did same thing. Now the canoe was grounded, but it was in the water enough that it'd be easy to undo what I'd just done when it was time to leave.

I untied the gray bag, the one with the cook gear, and then the green bag with the food, and went to work.

I filled the pot with water, lit the stove, which I thought was kind of a weird thing to do with fires already burning on both sides of me.

I ate some crackers and cheese while the water heated up. The warm wind from the fire combined with all the work I'd done to move the canoe and wrestle the dry bags out of the canoe left me feeling hot with sweat pouring out of me just about everywhere.

The adult moose were now half in the water in the main river, just standing there, with their little ones in up to their knees.

I shook my head. Moose don't look that smart, but I'd just learned something from them. I took my boots and socks off, unclipped my fanny pack which held a small survival kit, stripped off my pants and underwear, and then peeled off my T-shirt. I dropped my cap and bandana on top of my T-shirt and waded into the river just above the stern of the canoe. The water was surprisingly cold given what was burning on both shores. I took a deep breath and then sat in the river and then dunked my head under. I sat up but stayed in the river, just like the moose were doing, cooling off while a fire burned close by.

Both adult moose kept looking at me. One took a step in my direction, and that made my heart beat a little harder. It took another step. And then it turned its body sideways to me.

Okay, I thought. Why now? What was all-of-a-sudden different that was making the moose approach me? I scooted closer to the canoe so I was still in the water but only my head was visible over the side of the canoe.

By now, the second moose had taken a step toward me as well and had turned and sideways to me like the first moose had done. The two calves were sticking pretty close to their mothers, so they'd moved toward me as well.

"You can come as close as you want," I said softly. "Just don't stomp on me."

Like they could understand me, they moved a couple of steps closer, still facing sideways to me. Maybe they figured that for all the threat I might be, I was only worth being watched out of one eye.

Okay, I thought. Just go about my business. Keep it calm.

When I saw steam rising from the pot, I stood up. Yeah, I was naked but I didn't think the moose would care. I mean, they were naked, too. I walked slowly on the rocks and sand over to the stove, not wanting to startle the moose. The water was boiling. I turned off the stove and let the pot of water sit there.

Out of the corner of my eye, I checked in on the moose. They hadn't moved closer, but they hadn't moved farther away. I'd actually moved closer to them to deal with the stove.

More crackers and cheese, and then a couple of granola bars found their way down my throat as the water cooled and the moose stood still.

After the air had dried my skin, I got dressed, put my fanny pack on, soaked the bandana and tied it around my nose and mouth, and dunked my hat in the river and put it on. Then I filled my water bottles with the still-hot-but-not-boiling water. There was about a quart of water left in the pot, so I held the pot in the river to cool it, careful not to let the water from the river spill over the rim.

I tested it with my finger, and when it was lukewarm I took a long drink. I ate another granola bar and then drank the rest of the water in the pot. The moose were still in the water, just standing. And now their calves were standing closer to me than their mothers, which I thought was odd. I mean wouldn't the mothers want to be between their calves and a potential predator like myself?

Were they going to wait here on this tiny island until it was cool enough to go back to shore? If I didn't have a canoe, that's probably what I'd do. I'd just keep getting in the water to cool off until the fire passed and the land had cooled.

Were Billy and his dad sitting in the river too? Could Billy even get his dad to the river? Had the cabin burned up or had the metal roof protected it? Was the fire burning there right now? I wished I had a crystal ball so I could see what was happening. So I could know how they were and what they were dealing with. So I could know if my best friend was okay. I wished I had a two-way radio so I could tell Billy that even though we'd had some angry words at the cabin, I was still doing everything I could to get help.

I put two more Clif Bars in my back pocket, put one water bottle in my dry bag and the other loose in the boat, checked my fanny pack buckle to make sure it had clicked closed, and then repacked the rest of the canoe.

Knowing I might not be out of the boat again for hours, I peed, stretched my legs and arms, and flexed my ankle. I lifted the bow of the canoe into the water, ran to the stern, edged it in, and when the current started to tug the canoe, I pushed off and jumped in.

I dug my paddle into the water on the right side so the boat would move left, away from the moose.

I took a couple more paddle strokes and now, as my boat drifted out toward the center of the river, I saw why the moose had moved toward me.

# AT THE CABIN

## [TWO DAYS BEFORE THE FIRE]

It looked like a bear, only smaller, as it charged toward us. And bear cubs don't charge; they run away and cry and let their mothers take care of business.

A patch of tan fur ran across its forehead, contrasting with the dark brown of the rest of the animal.

I pointed the canister of bear spray toward the animal and pressed down on the trigger. A whooshing sound drowned out the constant snarls of the animal while a red fog shot out of the can.

Wolverine, I thought. That's a wolverine. And I felt the sweat building on my arms and legs, everywhere. They were known to chase wolves and bears off of carcasses.

The wolverine slowed when it reached the edge of the red fog and turned toward the river. It splashed in the shallows.

Billy had stopped cutting into the moose and was watching.

"Finish cutting that piece of meat," I said. "Then let's go—fast!"

The wolverine was swimming downstream and angling toward shore just below us. Out of the corner of my eye, I saw Billy cutting into the moose.

Water pouring off its fur, the wet wolverine charged out of the shallows toward the carcass.

I jumped over the moose and pointed the canister toward the wolverine.

I pressed the trigger again, this time for longer, and the red fog formed a bigger barrier. The wolverine veered toward the river, avoiding the red cloud, and started swimming upriver.

"It's dodging the bear spray. Just changing its course to the carcass. Whatever you got," I yelled to Billy, "let's go!"

I kept my eye on the wolverine as we moved upriver, the same direction it was taking in the water but it was the only way we could go because of the bluff downriver.

I heard Billy breathing heavy behind me. "Go," he said. "Faster!"

The wolverine was splashing through the water toward shore now, almost even with us. The moose carcass was fifty feet behind us. The wolverine had learned in an instant to avoid the red cloud of bear spray.

The beast crashed through the shallows and, instead of claiming the carcass like I hoped it would, charged straight at us. I stopped and pointed the bear spray in its direction. I pulled the trigger, and a small, weak cloud of red fog shot out, and then there was nothing.

It was empty.

And the wolverine kept coming.

# CHAPTER 17

**THE BLACK** bear was on the small side compared to the moose. But still, a bear is a bear. It was on the tip of the island at the edge of the trees. The four moose moved up the island and occupied the spot I'd vacated, giving the bear a little more space.

The bear waded into the water until all four legs were half submerged in the current. It had a bare spot about the size of a basketball on its back.

A burn? I thought.

Maybe.

And seeing the bear and moose so close together made me think about how they might work things out, because usually when a bear sees a moose calf, it tries to kill and eat it and the moose defend their young.

But in this case, the bear might say, *hey all you moose, I won't bother any of you if you won't bother me. Let's just make it through this fire. I already got burned once.*

And one of the moose might say back, *you keep up your end of the agreement and we'll keep ours.*

And the bear might say, *okay, but this deal ends as soon as the fire's out.*

And all of the moose would shout, *duh!*

I kept paddling, wanting to see the wide Tanana River appearing in the smoke.

The primary color on the shore to the right was black, like maybe I was getting into a section of fire that had burned a couple days ago. But on the left side, it was more active. There were pockets of flames.

*Stay in the water.*

"Tell me something new, or shut up," I said.

Even though the fire seemed less intense, the smoke was just as thick, if not thicker. I wished I had some goggles or a ski mask—something to protect my eyes and seal them off from the nasty air. But the smoke made things dim, too, and I needed all the light my eyes could gather so I could pick which side of the river to be on and hopefully avoid sweepers and other obstacles.

I rounded another bend and encountered a distinct waterline where the clear water of the Olsen merged with the gray-brown of the Tanana.

Fifty miles, I thought. I'd traveled about fifty miles and I hadn't flipped the canoe and drowned. And it'd taken about a day and a half.

I was relieved to put the Olsen behind me, to have successfully paddled fifty miles on the small, swift, winding river, but at the same time I was nervous about getting on to the bigger river. I was just getting used to the Olsen and now I had to deal with something new.

I wasn't just nervous. I was scared. I had hoped I wouldn't even have to paddle this far before running into people. My stomach tightened up and I felt a burning sensation at the base of my throat. It was mostly luck that I'd made it this far without drowning. The silty gray-brown water of the bigger river could swallow me in an instant.

"There's lots of channels in the Tanana," Mr. Dodge had managed to tell me in a weak voice despite his injuries. "Sometimes more than half a dozen to choose from. Try to stay in the main ones. The sloughs, the ones off to the sides, barely have a current, and can wind for miles through the forest."

I remembered how in the motorboat on the way to the cabin Mr. Dodge had always been scouting as he drove, trying to pick the channel he wanted well in advance. He'd done a good job driving the motorboat.

Mr. Dodge had lost his cool a few times during the first couple of days at the cabin, but everything that happened on that day he told us to head up to where the Olsen Forks and wait for him was like a slow-motion disaster. Him throwing those pieces of firewood at Billy turned out to be the least troubling event of the day.

At their house in Fairbanks for the six months or so I'd lived with them, I saw Mr. Dodge get really angry a few times a month but only one time did he do something physical.

"I don't care if you don't like it," he'd shouted at Mrs. Dodge. "This is the way I'm doing it."

Billy started to edge his way out of the kitchen and I followed him but we both heard the sound of glass breaking and then the door slamming leading to the garage.

Billy faced toward me but kept his head down. "I'm sorry you had to see that."

I said, "I know your dad has a good side but he can be scary."

Billy looked me in the eye. "At least he's mostly switched from hitting people to just destroying stuff." Billy cracked a fake smile. "I'm going to go see if my mom's okay."

I refocused my thoughts on the river and what Mr. Dodge had said about it. At least if there are lots of channels, then there are lots of islands. And if there are fires raging next to the Tanana on the shore, then I'm going to need islands.

"Watch out for log jams," Mr. Dodge had said. "Sweepers, too. And, the Tanana's current is stronger than the Olsen's. And you never know what could be right below the surface because of the silt."

A little chill traveled up my spine. The clear water of the Olsen was completely gone from beneath the canoe. The charred right-shore was close by my side. I glanced across the river.

Wide.

Wide.

Wide.

Somewhere, in all that smoke was the opposite bank. And somewhere in the middle were probably channels and islands, and I knew if I just hugged the right bank I'd eventually get sucked into a slow-moving slough. That'd be the safe thing to do while traveling in a flimsy boat on a big river. That's what I wanted to do.

I pictured Billy and his dad trying to survive the fire. Then I pictured Billy's dad all groggy from his injuries and I knew in my heart what I needed to do even though my brain kept telling me to stick close to the shore.

I swallowed my fear and dug my paddle in on the right side, and the canoe responded, moving farther away from the shore. The river was moving along. Like I was on a high-powered conveyor belt of watery silt. My arms shook like I was shivering. But I wasn't shivering from being cold. It was fear. The Tanana was so much bigger and stronger than the

Olsen. If I ran into problems in the middle of the river and ended up in the water, the current would drag me under.

The silt in the water made a little noise, like distant, rusty, miniature wind chimes might make, as the thousands upon thousands of particles collided with the canoe.

I spotted a log bobbing in the current just above the surface and flared my paddle to turn the canoe. I glided by it but not before I noticed its jagged point.

I'd need to be extremely careful.

The gray brown water combined with the thick yellow smoke made for extra-poor visibility. And now, it was getting late and even though it wasn't going to get dark, the light was dimming as the sun, invisible to me, was probably nearing the horizon.

My eyes wanted to close. My legs wanted to stretch out. I let out a big yawn.

I'd need to find a place to stop for a little while.

*Stay in the water.*

"An island," I said. "Just like earlier today." I'll find an island, boil up some water, cook some noodles and wait out the darkest part of the night. Three or four hours tops.

I could see a line of trees in the middle of the river. The tops of some islands, I thought. The start of some channels. As I approached closer, I noticed driftwood piled up at the heads of the islands, like they were strainers catching anything and everything that floated downriver.

I back-paddled to buy myself a little more time because I didn't want to become the newest addition to one of those piles, but the current was super-strong and the boat didn't respond as quickly as it had on the Olsen.

I paddled forward, wanting to round the tip of the first island, trying to get on the left side of it. Trying to get to a channel that was more in the middle of the river. Because of the smoke, I could only see a couple hundred feet downriver, but I wasn't even looking there now.

I was focused on the mishmash of driftwood logs that I was trying to get around, paddling hard on the right, which was moving me left, which was where I wanted to go. I just wasn't moving left fast enough to avoid that sloppy, jagged pile of logs.

# AT THE CABIN
## [TWO DAYS BEFORE THE FIRE]

"The meat!" I yelled. "Throw it the meat."

Billy heaved a deep red-purple mass about half the size of a loaf of bread toward the wolverine and it thumped onto the ground. We started working our way up the hill toward the top of the bluff as fast as we could go, angling sideways to keep the wolverine in view.

The wolverine stopped when it got to the meat, spread its front legs over it, and with its head pointed in our direction sent out a low growl into the world. Then it grabbed the hunk of meat in its jaws, loped toward the carcass like it was carrying a feather, and scattered the ravens that had swept down on it when we had run.

On the top of the bluff, from the spot we'd watched the wolves dismantle the moose, we watched the wolverine do the same with what was left.

"I told you that going down there was a dumb thing to do." I shook my head.

Billy countered, "It was you who fired the Bear Spray too soon. If that wolverine would've taken a direct hit the first time it would've left. You should've let it get closer before you fired. Admit it."

"If I'd listened to myself instead of you," I responded, "I wouldn't have had to fire at all." I held up the cannister of bear spray. "It's empty."

"Okay," Billy said. "We both made some mistakes. At least we didn't get hurt." Billy paused. "When we tell my dad about our hike, let's skip the part about getting charged by a wolverine. If he's still in a bad mood, and he hears about that, it'll just give him a reason to stay in it. I've seen it happen before."

"Fine by me," I agreed. "I just want to get up to the forks."

"Tom, you said approaching the carcass was a bad idea." Billy grimaced. "If you felt that strongly about it, why'd you let me talk you into doing that?"

I replied, "I didn't want to let you down. I've been living with your family for months now. I—"

"I've stayed at your house plenty." Billy grabbed my shoulder and looked me in the eye. "You don't owe me anything. If you think something is a bad idea just say so." Then he let my shoulder go but kept looking at me.

"I'm glad your mom and dad let me live with you all these months. It's going to suck moving to Michigan with my uncle. I wish he didn't have so much power over my life."

"I tried to convince my parents to try to have you keep living with us, but my mom wouldn't go for that." Billy kicked the ground a couple of times. "It's going to suck for both of us."

I nodded but didn't say anything. Billy was right. Period.

We both turned our attention back to the wolverine.

It had chewed through the backbone and broken the moose into three sections. The little beast was just starting to drag the middle section farther from the water when it stopped and looked upstream. I followed the wolverine's gaze and saw movement in the river upstream from the kill site.

"Billy." I pointed upstream. "Look."

A small blond bear with a hump on its back emerged from the river and shook the excess water off its fur like a dog. The wolverine remained by the carcass, but let out a snarl and crouched down, ready to defend its prize.

# CHAPTER 18

**I DID** a sweeping back-paddle on the left, and that swung the bow out just as it was about to collide with the logs. Then I dug my paddle in on the right and pulled, but I'd run of out of space between the canoe and the logjam.

I lifted my paddle out of the water and pushed it into the logjam, trying to keep the canoe from getting pinned. The current was pulling on the bow of the canoe, which had cleared the jam. The canoe caught for a second and then kept sliding downstream, but not without a cost.

A ripping, screeching sound invaded my ears and then the canoe floated free, but I needed to get to shore.

There was now a foot-long tear next to my right thigh.

Water splashed in as a small wave bumped against the canoe.

"No!" I yelled, as more and more water splashed in.

An image of our accident off the shore of Bear Island where I'd barely escaped drowning filled my mind as I dug my paddle in and pulled for shore.

A bigger wave poured more water through the hole. There was no way to keep the river out of the boat. My heart was beating so hard it was going to break a hole in my chest and fly to shore without me.

Below the logjam I dug my paddle into the water and steered the canoe toward shore. I jumped out in thigh-high water and the silty river poured into my boots and tried to drag me downriver. I held the side of the canoe and kept my footing. The only thing that mattered was feeling the ground underneath my feet.

I sloshed across the current and got the canoe to a sandy spot on the island. Then I alternated lifting the bow and then the stern until the whole boat was sitting above the superhighway of silty water.

My whole body shook. I sat down on the shore and sucked in a breath through my bandana. I just wanted to wait here until someone came or until I died. Anything but being on the river.

It was at least a quarter mile across to the mainland from where I was. The smoke made the land across the river look like it was fading away. The big silty mess of the Tanana River kept flowing on-by a few feet from where I was sitting, not caring whether my boat was floatable or not.

The river didn't take sides.

It wasn't there to help me.

It wasn't there to hurt me.

It was just there.

But it was huge. And just being what it was, it could kill me.

I glanced at the tear in the side of the canoe. One stranded log of thousands had done that.

"Well, River," I said. "I know you don't care. But I do. I care."

I picked up a rock and threw it into the river as hard as I could, and yelled, "I care!"

I tugged my boots off, emptied them of silty water, rung out my socks and then everything back on. I didn't have time to dry anything out because as much as I wanted to just sit here, I knew I couldn't. I couple of tears escaped. I wiped them away.

Then I turned my attention to the canoe.

The tear was pretty clean, not jagged and messy. But still, it was a tear in the side of the canoe.

A hole in a boat is not a good thing.

I looked at the river again. Thousands of gallons of water a second flowing by. It'd been doing this for a long time. A lot of logjams had formed and then been washed away, but the river had kept going. It was my ticket out of this fire-scorched land. It was my ticket to getting help for Billy and Mr. Dodge. It was my ticket to be able to live the rest of my life and not die from drowning, my lungs filling with silty water but I wished it would just go away. Sitting in a motorboat while Mr. Dodge was driving was one thing, but me, alone in a flimsy canoe with a big hole was another.

I swallowed down my fear and turned my head back toward the canoe and the tear.

"I need to fix you," I said.

I knelt in the sand and studied the hole. It was a straight tear running parallel with the canoe lengthwise and about a foot long. It was a little more than halfway down from the rim of the canoe. And it sat right next to where I knelt.

You could see the tan of the birch ribs of the canoe through the hole. They pressed tightly against the skin of the canoe and seemed to have bulged out a bit where the tear was. It was like the skin had kept the ribs from expanding and now that they had a chance they were taking it.

Repair kit, I thought. "I don't have one," I said. "At least not officially."

But somehow, I had to do something to keep the river out of the boat.

My mind tore into the problem as I untied my dry bags and set them on shore, emptying out the canoe of everything except the ballast rocks in the bow of the boat.

I stared at the pile of gear. "There's got to be a way to plug that hole."

But I didn't want just any way. I wanted the best way. The way that would hold up in waves and in the constant push of the river. The way that would keep me from drowning.

Yes, I wanted the best way, but also a fast way. For Billy and Mr. Dodge. If it had been just me, I could have taken my time and really done a good job. I had food, a stove, a tent. I had everything, except time.

Time, I now realized, was the most dangerous factor on this trip. The clock on Mr. Dodge's injuries was ticking, and that was putting pressure on me. Pressure to work quickly, to take as few breaks as possible, so I could keep following the river. Pressure to push my fears to the side and stay on the water. I'd done okay on the smaller river but on the Tanana I'd barely paddled and already I'd had an accident. But a bigger pressure now was the fire. Billy and his dad could be burned alive if I didn't get help to them in time. I felt the smoky air pressing on me from every direction. There was no relief anywhere. Relentless pressure.

Pressure, I thought. What about pressure? I stared at the hole, my mind churning away at the problem.

Pressure.

The ribs and the fabric exerted a pressure on each other, and I needed to make that pressure work for me.

# AT THE CABIN

## [TWO DAYS BEFORE THE FIRE]

A small blond bear with a hump on its back emerged from the river and shook the excess water off its fur like a dog would. The wolverine remained by the carcass, but let out a snarl and crouched down, ready to defend its prize.

The young grizzly advanced, halving the distance between it and the carcass before stopping and standing on its hind legs. It wagged its head back and forth.

The wolverine let out a long snarl but didn't budge from its position.

Even though I wasn't involved in the stand-off below, my heart was beating overtime, like it had its own memories of all the times I'd fended off bears out on Bear Island.

The grizzly was back on all four legs now, advancing slowly. The wolverine snarled again and positioned itself squarely between the bear and the carcass.

"Who fights a grizzly?" Billy whispered, his eyes glued to the drama below.

I just hoped the loser, whichever it turned out to be, wouldn't come running this way. I knew that the safest thing to do would be to leave, but I couldn't drag my eyes away from what was happening. Plus, movement might draw attention to us, and I didn't want that either.

Now about ten feet separated the bear from the wolverine. The bear took another step forward, and the wolverine sprang into action, attacking low and hard. The bear dodged the attack and approached the carcass from another angle, but the wolverine came at it again, showing it had no problem with trying to sink its teeth into something six times its size.

I kept waiting for the bear to swat it out of the way with one of its paws, but the wolverine never gave it a chance. That bear was always defending itself from the wolverine lunging at its legs and hind section. It drove the bear farther from the carcass and didn't let up until the bear splashed its way across the river and disappeared in the forest on the other side.

"It's not that big," Billy said, "but it sure is tough." The wolverine had returned to the carcass and was dragging the mid-section farther from shore, like it'd been doing before the bear appeared.

"We should head for the forks while that beast," I pointed down at the wolverine, "is still busy."

# CHAPTER 19

**I LIFTED** the ballast rocks out of the bow and set them on the ground. I carefully turned the canoe on its side and then all the way over so the water that had splashed and poured through the hole could drain out. Then I turned the canoe back over.

I uncapped my water bottle, lifted the bandana covering my face, and took a long drink. I wished the smoke would clear. Even if only for a few hours. Or for a few seconds. One breath of fresh air, that's all I wanted. One normal thing in this crazy chain of events that was currently my life.

The hole in the canoe seemed to be smiling at me. Like it was saying, *Got you now, Tom. What are you going to do?*

"Fix you," I said to the canoe. "I will fix you. I don't know how yet, but I'll do it. With pressure."

I tapped the ribs that were visible through the tear. Then I worked the tip of my index finger between a rib and the fabric. "Tight fit," I said. But still, a hole is a hole. I needed to fix it and fix it fast.

I opened my yellow dry bag and dumped out the contents on the gravel bar.

First aid kit
Pile jacket
Bag of peanuts
Water bottle
Raincoat
Rain pants

From the red stuff sack, I removed the Ziploc bags from the first aid kit. Band Aids, ace bandage, bottle of aspirin, tube of Neosporin, and gauze pads.

My eyes focused in on the ace bandage. If only it were waterproof. Then I glanced at my raincoat and rain pants.

Rain, I thought. If it rained, I'd kiss the sky. I'd kiss everything. Fresh water to wash the smoke away. I picked up my rain pants and stretched out one leg and held it tight.

Wide enough, I thought.

Taking the bottom of one leg, I worked the fabric under the ribs of the canoe a couple of inches forward from where the tear started. It was slow and tedious work inching the fabric toward the hole and spreading it out so it reached above and below the tear. The blue nylon was smooth, but that didn't prevent it from getting caught on small rough spots on the ribs.

When I reached the opening where the hole began, the work went a little quicker. With one hand I gripped the end of the pant leg, which was now sticking out of the hole, and grabbed the rim of the canoe with my other hand for leverage.

I gave the leg a pull, and more of the fabric emerged from the hole, so I kept pulling until I had enough fabric hanging free to cover the hole plus a few more inches to weave back under the ribs beyond where the tear ended.

I stood up and stretched my back and then took another drink of water, emptying the bottle. I looked at the other bottle. It was full, but then what would I drink? I glanced at the silty water trucking by the gravel bar.

I couldn't count on finding a clear stream because I didn't know this country. And it wasn't like Bear Island where it rained all the time, and clear, clean streams tumbled into the ocean everywhere you looked.

Then I remembered a science experiment we'd done in school a couple years ago where we'd collected silty water and let it sit in a jar until the silt sank to the bottom so we could see how much silt was actually in the water.

I opened the gray dry bag, took out the pot, dipped it in the river and filled it up.

Let the silt settle, I thought, while I finish the repair job.

I put the pot down on a level spot, knelt next to the canoe and started working the blue nylon under the ribs. The fabric on this side of the hole seemed tighter than where I'd started on the opposite side, so it was harder to get the nylon to move.

Pressure, pressure, pressure, my mind kept saying over and over.

The tips of my fingers ached from all the pushing and pulling, but I finally got the slack out. The blue patch covered the hole, held tight by the pressure between the fabric and the ribs.

Inside the canoe, the rest of the rain pants lay just beneath where I'd started shoving the fabric through. Instead of cutting the rest of the pants away, I decided to let them stay attached to the patch in case I needed to pull more of the fabric through the hole. Plus, there was no real reason to cut them away. If I had to beach the boat and walk, and by some miracle it turned cold and rained, then I'd still have rain pants to wear.

I turned my attention to the pot of water, and out of the corner of my eye caught movement down the gravel bar about two hundred feet from me. Something was crawling out of the river.

# AT THE CABIN

## [TWO DAYS BEFORE THE FIRE]

We had reached the spot where the Olsen River forks and were standing on a gravel bar at the edge of the river.

Billy slipped off his backpack and pulled a collapsible fishing rod out of it. "My dad said this is as far as a motorboat can go and I can see why."

The mouth of the left fork ran strong with water tumbling over and flowing between big blocky boulders. The mouth of the right fork was flatter water, but just upstream you could see boulders poking above the surface, ready to snag any motorboat that tried to move through.

I wondered where the wolves, wolverine, and bear we had seen were now. I set my empty canister of bear spray on the ground and took my backpack off.

"I'm going fishing," Billy cut into my thoughts. "If we can—"

*Owuuuuuu!*

Billy and I both peered across the river.

*Owuuuuuu!*

Another wolf answered from a different direction and a chill shot up my spine.

I stared upriver toward where the second call had come from, trying to see shapes in the thick forest that surrounded us. "I don't see anything," I said. "But you can bet they've seen us."

"I want to know where they are," Billy said.

"At least with two of us we're less likely to be attacked, but if we're going to wait here for your dad, we'll need to show them that we're staking out our territory."

"For real?" Billy asked.

"I don't know exactly," I replied. "But if we act all scared, it'll show them that they're in charge and then they'll be more likely to view us as a potential food source. We have to show them that we *live* here, too. We should build a fire." I slapped a mosquito that was starting to suck blood from my cheek. "The smoke will keep the mosquitos away, too."

"If that's what we've got to do, stake out our territory," Billy smirked, "then let's do what my dog used to do." Billy backed up a few steps, and turned so he was facing away." He glanced over his shoulder and said, "What are you waiting for? Pick a spot and get busy."

I laughed, but if dogs marked their territories, then why couldn't we? I walked a few steps in the opposite direction that Billy walked, unzipped my zipper and peed.

*Owuuuuuu!*

I zipped back up, turned a slow circle, but saw nothing.

We stripped some birch bark from a tree, picked up sticks and built a small fire on the edge of the gravel bar.

"If we catch a fish," Billy said, "we could cook it up on the fire." He added another stick to the flames. "Remember when we cooked hotdogs on a fire with your Mom and Dad?"

"How could I forget?" I smiled. "You almost burned the woods down behind my house." Billy had dumped way too many sticks on the fire and some sparks had shot out and caught some dry leaves on fire.

"Your dad was so laid back about the whole thing." Billy stood up and took a step toward me. "Grab that bucket of water," he said, imitating my dad, "before that fire spreads."

I laughed. "Sounds just like him."

I watched Billy cast his line and reel it in a couple of times. Then I added a few more sticks to the fire.

The sun was touching the treetops. I glanced at my watch. As much as I liked just hanging out with Billy and not being subjected to Mr. Dodge and his unpredictable mood swings, I was starting to get worried about him.

# CHAPTER 20

## SIX WOLVES in all.

Another family fleeing the fire, I thought, just like the fox and the moose.

Each of them had shaken the water off their fur when they'd emerged from the river onto the island where I had just patched my canoe.

An image of the wolves Billy and I had seen take down that moose and eat it alive filled my brain.

I was way smaller than a moose.

*Keep packing up.*

Wolves almost never attacked humans.

Almost.

There's only been one recent known wolf attack on a person in Alaska. A few years ago, a teacher working in a remote village went out for a run by herself and didn't come back. Her partially eaten body was found with wolf tracks all around it.

I started to repack the bow of the boat. I put the ballast rocks in. I tossed all the dry bags in except the gray one because my pot of water was still sitting on the ground.

A bark from one of the wolves turned my attention back toward them. Through the yellow haze I could see them, standing shoulder to shoulder, facing me.

My arms trembled as I dumped the water, tossed the pot in the gray dry bag and put in it the boat.

I swallowed the lump of fear in my throat, lifted the bow of the boat, and walked sideways a few steps and set it into the river.

Then I lifted the stern and walked the canoe into the river until it floated. I glanced back at the gravel bar one last time. I hadn't left any of my gear.

I hopped in the canoe and knelt. I did a couple of hard paddle strokes on the right side of the canoe, and that swung me into the current, and within seconds I was even with the wolves, who were yipping and barking.

"Okay," I said. "You can have the island."

One of the wolves took a step toward me and the others followed. My eyes were glued to them as I picked up the pace with my paddling. When their front legs were half-covered in water they stopped.

I let out a breath I didn't know I was holding and then turned my attention downstream. At least I was back on the river moving in the right direction.

Nothing like a little a fear to keep you awake, I thought. I was dead tired, but now I was also wired. And to paddle this river through the thick smoke in this fragile boat, I needed to be wired—all the time. My fear of getting eaten alive overrode my fear of being on the river. But now that I was back on the river and the wolves were gone, my fear of drowning crept back in.

I glanced down at the blue patch. The canoe sat in the water so the bottom of the blue patch just touched the top of the river, but sometimes a small wave would wash over it and the patch would totally submerge. The boat was wet on the inside just below the patch, like maybe a little bit of water had worked its way in from the bottom of the patch.

My throat was bone dry. I'd put both my water bottles in the dry bag when I'd packed up in a hurry. I didn't see any obstacles downriver that I had to deal with in the next minute or two so I leaned forward and grabbed the yellow dry bag.

As I opened the bag I realized that none of the bags were tied in, so if the canoe flipped I'd lose everything except the fanny pack with the survival kit that I was wearing.

I found the full water bottle, unscrewed the lid and took a long drink. I dug around until I found the bag of peanuts, ate a few handfuls, and drank some more water.

Downriver, a line of trees appeared to be forming across the water.

Islands, I thought. And with islands, there'd be channels to choose from. I felt a shiver travel up my spine. Whatever channel I picked I'd try to stay in the middle of it. But somewhere, hopefully soon, I wanted to land the boat so I could secure the dry bags.

I stuck the peanuts back in the dry bag. The water bottle I kept out.

A little chop was forming on the water—small waves bumped into the canoe and rode up on it. And when that happened on the back-right side, the patch would get totally submerged in the silty water.

I kept paddling, but I could see what was happening. There was a little puddle in the canoe just back from my right knee.

I needed a way to make the back of the canoe ride higher in the water.

As I approached the line of tree-covered islands, I saw that most of the trees weren't really trees anymore.

The islands were a smoking haze of mostly charred giant spruce snags with some birches that hadn't burnt all the way. The fire must've leap-frogged across the islands. I remembered the red embers I'd seen blowing across the Olsen, starting fires on the opposite side of the river.

My mind worked on the problem of the patch sitting too low in the water while at the same I tried to stay focused on choosing a channel to get me through the charred islands.

Fire.

Water.

Fire.

Water.

I had two problems. Usually water would protect you from fire. But in my case if water sank my canoe, then I'd be forced to face the fires raging on shore, that is, if I didn't drown.

I dug my paddle into the water and guided the canoe a little to the left. My approach centered me on a channel running between the middle two of the four charred islands I'd counted.

The puddle next to my leg had grown larger. I needed to lift the back of the canoe up. I needed it to ride higher. The more water the canoe took on, the lower it would ride. And the lower the canoe rode, the more water it would take on.

And then I had an idea, but I needed to land the canoe to try it.

# AT THE CABIN

## [TWO DAYS BEFORE THE FIRE]

"It's almost midnight." I put my hands in front of the fire. Billy had fished for a while but hadn't caught anything.

"Even in one of his moods," Billy said, "my dad wouldn't want us out here all night. Maybe he ran into problems."

We talked some more and decided to hike the six miles back to the cabin, figuring that if we stayed by the river there's no way we could miss him if he's motoring toward us.

I stood up. "We'll have to go up and over the bluff, but we'll be able to see the river and call down if your dad is in the boat." I picked up the empty canister of bear spray. "We'll have to be extra careful when we get near that carcass, whatever is left of it."

"Don't worry." Billy grinned. "I won't be going any closer than I have to."

We drank the last of the water in our water bottles and then filled them with river water and dumped them on the fire. We refilled the bottles four or five times, turning the fire into an ashy mud pit. It had been a pretty dry summer so far and we didn't want any stray coals to start a forest fire.

Once the mosquitoes figured out there was no more smoke, they came at us like heat seeking missiles. We started walking, keeping the pace fast enough so the little bloodsuckers had a hard time landing on us.

As we walked, I hoped the wolves and wolverine we'd seen earlier were all well fed from the moose carcass. And I hoped that the bear was still on the other side of the river.

*Just don't look like prey. Don't even let a predator think that you're potentially something to eat.*

At least there were two of us out here. That alone would make it less likely that a bear or a wolverine or wolves would try to make a meal out of us. But there were no guarantees.

A little while later on top of the bluff, we looked down through the dim light and watched a pair of red fox feeding on the remains of the moose carcass.

After a couple of minutes Billy said, "We should keep going."

We worked our way down the bluff and then stuck close to the river as we headed back toward the cabin. I was hungry but we'd eaten all of the Clif Bars and cheese and crackers. In the distance I could see the sun just starting to rise. I peeked at my watch. It read just after 2:30.

Billy was about ten feet in front of me trucking along, and I just got into the rhythm of following him and we put a few more miles behind us. We were walking faster than we had on the hike out to the forks.

It was around 4:00 a.m. when we heard a faint cry for help.

# CHAPTER 21

I STEERED clear of the piles of driftwood on the upstream side of the islands and entered the channel. I didn't know when the fire had torn through here. I didn't even know which direction it had taken when it jumped the river. The wolves I'd encountered on the last island had swum from the left bank, so I'd assumed the fire had chased them into the river, but I didn't know for sure.

I mean, the smoke was so thick, and everywhere I looked there was burnt forest.

I felt a little moisture in my right boot and glanced downward. Enough water had gathered in the canoe that some of it had flowed into my boot.

My feet were already wet, so I didn't care about that. What I cared about was that more and more water was working its way into the canoe.

An old canoe.

Made of sticks and fabric.

A canoe with a big hole in it.

A leaky, damaged canoe on a relentless river.

A sandy beach came into view on the island off to the left, so I steered toward it. If my idea worked, then I wouldn't have to be as worried about the boat filling up with water from the hole I'd patched. I'd still have to worry about running into sweepers or poking and ripping new holes in the boat, but I'd been worrying about all that since I'd taken my first paddle stroke downriver.

But to fix the patched hole I needed it to ride higher in the water. Weight, I thought. It's all about weight and where you put it.

By the narrow strip of sandy beach, I hopped out of the canoe and pulled it ashore, thankful for the smooth sand that wouldn't damage the bottom of the boat. I slid the canoe about ten feet up the beach. The huge burnt-up trees, just back from the beach, greeted me with some creaking noises as a gust of wind blew through them. I glanced up at the dead giants and then got the pot out of the gray bag, filled it with water, and set it on a level spot so the silt could settle to the bottom while I worked on the canoe.

I knew what I wanted to do to move the weight around, but since I had the boat onshore and there didn't appear to be any wolves coming my way, I examined the patch. The nylon felt tight, like the water should bounce off it. Maybe the problem was that I didn't really have it sealed where the nylon met the canoe fabric, so water penetrated the canoe on the borders of the patch or maybe the fabric wasn't totally waterproof.

"Enough," I said. I could stare at it all day, but that wouldn't make it waterproof. I didn't see an easy way to make it better, so I focused on what to try to keep the patch from riding so low in the water.

First, I moved the two dry bags in the middle of the canoe up to the bow. Next, I took the yellow dry bag I used as a seat and the yellow dry bag that held food, water, and rain gear and moved them to the center of the canoe, leaving the stern totally empty. Then I moved my knee pads up to the center of the canoe.

I was the heaviest thing in the canoe and I hoped moving me up to the middle would make the stern ride a little higher and keep the patch out of the water.

I wasn't sure how sitting in the middle of the canoe would be for paddling and steering, but if the canoe filled with water and sank, then there would be no canoe for paddling and steering, and I'd be walking. And right now, from what I was seeing, there was a good chance I'd be burned alive if I had to walk.

I wanted to get the water out of the boat, so I unloaded all the dry bags and ballast rocks, tipped the canoe over and drained the water that had come in through the hole. Then, I repacked the canoe minus the ballast rocks because I needed the boat to be lighter. I secured all the dry bags in the bow with rope and clipped the small yellow dry bag on the strut in front of my new position in the middle of the canoe. I put the big yellow dry bag in the center of the canoe and set my kneepads on either side of it.

I glanced around the beach and spotted the pot full of water and sighed. One more thing to deal with. The silt had mostly settled to the bottom of the pot. I found my water bottles, drank what was left and then carefully refilled them, trying to keep the silt from making its way into the bottles. The water in the bottles wasn't as clear as what I'd drunk while on the Olsen, but it wasn't as silty as the river in front of me.

Would drinking it without boiling it make me sick and give me diarrhea?

"Whatever," I said. "Like I've got a choice right now."

I stuffed the pot and one of the water bottles into the yellow dry bag. I ate another couple handfuls of peanuts and drank some of the water. I rubbed my tongue across my teeth, trying to erase the silt that had stuck to them.

Silt and smoke, I thought. This is the trip of silt and smoke. I soaked my bandana in the river, rung it out and tied it around my mouth and nose.

I turned toward the canoe just as a strong gust of wind blew across the beach and blasted me with sand. I squinted. I rubbed my eyes—not sure what was irritating them more, the sand or the smoke.

The wind continued to blow as I held the side of the canoe, my head tilted downward.

Add sand, I thought.

"The trip of smoke, silt, and sand," I said. I knew there was a song here. A song my mother would have liked, but I'd have to work on it later.

"Sing with me," I remembered my mom saying. It was just the two of us a few weeks before she was killed. "I'll teach you the chorus of my new song and then we can sing it for your dad when he gets home."

*Keep yourself open.*

*Keep yourself open.*

*Keep yourself open and see what comes your way.*

No matter where I ended up, whether I ran away or moved to Michigan with my uncle, I was taking my mom's guitar with me so I could keep playing her songs and keep writing new ones. I hadn't written any since I'd returned from Bear Island but knew I would in the future.

Another gust of wind blasted me.

Creaking noises invaded my ears, and I looked up at the line of burnt trees towering over me behind the beach. The wind was pushing on them. The remains of one big spruce was swaying more than the others.

A popping, screeching sound drowned out the creaking noises.

Then the big spruce snag started to lean, and gravity took over from there.

Falling.

It was falling toward me.

And my canoe.

# AT THE CABIN

## [ONE DAY BEFORE THE FIRE]

"I did a number on my leg. Hurts like the devil." Mr. Dodge gasped. "Probably broke it."

Billy knelt beside his dad. "What happened?"

"I got the motor going," Mr. Dodge said softly, "and started heading upriver." He took a breath and winced. His face was covered with red welts from mosquito bites. "The motor died as I was going around this bend." Mr. Dodge pointed to the river. "The boat drifted back into a sweeper." He rubbed his forehead. "Then it tipped and filled with water and then sunk, and I was in the water stuck between the boat and the sweeper." Mr. Dodge paused again. "My head was under and I was wrenching my body and somehow I got free but for a price." Mr. Dodge touched his leg. "Between the boat and the tree trunk, and me twisting and pushing and pulling, I think I busted my lower leg. I kicked and tugged my way to the shore and crawled out."

Billy put his hand on his dad's arm. "We'll get you back to the cabin." Billy looked at me.

I knelt next to Billy and said, "We should each get under a shoulder and lift."

"The gun." Mr. Dodge pointed upriver to some brush. "I threw it ashore just before the boat flipped."

Then I realized that the sweeper that had swallowed the boat must be right in front of us. I looked at the river and sure enough, stretching out into the water was a massive spruce tree. Somewhere under there was our boat.

Billy stood up and walked toward where his dad had pointed, rustled around in the brush, and then lifted the long gun to show he'd found it.

"Is the safety still on?" Mr. Dodge asked.

"Yes," Billy said.

"Don't put your hand anywhere near the trigger," Mr. Dodge said.

My mind flashed back to all the predators we'd seen. I was glad that moose-kill was upriver a few miles because Mr. Dodge would've been easy prey before we came along.

Mr. Dodge got himself into a sitting position, and we planted ourselves on opposite sides of him. On the count of three we all stood with Mr. Dodge putting his arms around me and Billy at the shoulders. Since Billy was a few inches shorter than me Mr. Dodge was leaning more toward him.

"Mr. Dodge," I said. "Lean toward me so I can take more of your weight and even things out."

Mr. Dodge shifted his weight and cried out in pain.

The mosquitoes figured out we were tied up with something other than killing them and started biting in earnest. I used my free arm to wipe my face clean of the vampires but they seemed to know we could only focus on them for so long.

"I can't put any weight on my right leg," Mr. Dodge said. "If you kids hadn't been such a pain this morning, none of this would've happened."

Billy must've known that now wasn't the time to argue because he responded only by saying, "We'll get you back to the cabin, Dad."

"That's right," I chimed in. "Just pretend we're your crutches." Even though Mr. Dodge was over six feet tall and heavily built, we'd do it. I just hoped he wouldn't blow his top on the way.

Billy and I took turns carrying the gun with our free hands, and two hours later we finally saw the cabin coming into view. My arms and legs were rubber and my back ached.

Another hundred yards and we could settle Mr. Dodge onto his bunk and deal with his injury. We thought we were done with the worst of it, but really, our troubles had just begun.

# CHAPTER 22

**IT SEEMED** to come toward me in slow motion at first, but then gained momentum.

*Save yourself. Now.*

I dove to my left and rolled past the stern of the canoe, covering my head with my arms.

The beach shook under me as a gigantic thump met my ears. There was another noise, too. An abrupt screeching sound, that came and went as quickly as the thump. As quickly as the beach shaking. As quickly as I'd rolled away.

I knew the wind was still blowing, because now that I was lying on the beach I could feel the sand hitting my arms, which were still covering my head.

I opened my eyes and sat up.

The charred trunk of the spruce sat partially sunk in the sand.

And the end of the trunk had pinned my canoe to the beach.

I jumped up and ran to the bow of the canoe.

"No," I said.

No!

No!

No!

Stupid luck.

Dumb luck.

Not really luck at all.

Just chance. But what was chance, really?

Did things just happen and you basically had no control over them? Or, did your actions matter?

Or, was the truth somehow somewhere in between the two? You could do your best to prepare and that might help you avoid some catastrophes. And planning might keep you from making some mistakes that you would have made.

But that didn't mean that everything would always work out.

That didn't mean that bad stuff still wouldn't happen.

That didn't mean that you wouldn't find yourself out of luck in the middle of river surrounded by fire.

That didn't mean that you could feel lucky because the falling tree had missed crushing you even though it hadn't missed your canoe.

# AT THE CABIN
## [ONE DAY BEFORE THE FIRE]

At the base of the steps, we paused. I doubled up on my support of Mr. Dodge while Billy set the gun down and took his pack off . When he was back in position, I slipped my pack off.

"Looks like the door is a little bit open," I said.

"The latch needs adjusting. The wind could've blown it open partway. Hopefully the squirrels haven't gotten inside." Mr. Dodge responded. "None of this would've happened if you two could've entertained yourselves around here and just stayed out of my way." On the hike back to the cabin, Mr. Dodge had blamed us for heading to the forks when it had been his idea. I just didn't understand that, but I hadn't tried to argue with him either.

I just wanted to get him inside and resting on his bunk so we could figure out what to do next now that the boat was gone.

Plus, my legs were spent from bearing a lot of his weight. Billy hadn't said much in the last hour or so. He had to be just as exhausted as I was.

Mr. Dodge put his good foot on the first step and Billy and I both moved forward and up onto the first step as well. Mr. Dodge's injured leg hung free, the tip of his boot barely touching the ground. I took a breath, readying myself for taking on the added pressure as we climbed the next of six steps.

On the count of three, me and Billy pushed upward and got ourselves and Mr. Dodge's good leg onto the second step. We did it two more times and now we were on the fourth step with just two more to go.

On the count of three we pushed upward but all of a sudden, a wall of black fur burst through the door and barreled down the steps right at us. I leaped sideways as the bear brushed by me. I stumbled off the edge of the steps and landed flat on my back.

I heard a groan and slowly sat up. At the base of the steps I could see Mr. Dodge lying on his back and Billy on the far side of him.

"Tom," Billy yelled, "get over here and help me."

# CHAPTER 23

**THE END** of the charred trunk, about as big around as my arm, sat on the now broken rim of the canoe about two feet from the tip of the bow.

"Okay," I said. "Okay." And no, this wasn't okay. But it was what I had to deal with.

*You can fix this. I know you can.*

On Bear Island, I hadn't had a boat to fix. Our kayak had been smashed to pieces as the waves pounded it against a huge razor-sharp rock formation.

My fault. That accident. For months, as I searched for my father, I'd struggled with it being my fault. All my fault.

But this? It was nobody's fault.

Now I couldn't even walk to get help. I looked at the river. I wouldn't last long if I tried to swim all the way to shore, I thought. And if I did make it, I might get burned up and die.

"Okay," I said again. "Use your brain to solve the problem."

I focused on the canoe. My only option was to try to fix it. The trunk had it pinned down.

I took in a big breath and the bandana closed in around my lips like it was trying to seal my mouth off, but then when I exhaled it released.

I've got to fix it, I thought. And I've got to fix it fast.

No. Not only fast. I've got to fix it so it'll last at least another hundred and fifty miles.

I grabbed the end of the trunk that was hanging off the broken rim in the middle of the canoe and lifted, but it didn't budge. The weight of the entire tree that had fallen wasn't cooperating.

"Come on." I tried lifting it again. Nothing.

My throat was tight. Like not only was the smoke bothering it, but it was being constricted from the inside. Like my body was attacking itself.

I swallowed a couple of times and took in a breath though my nose.

One of my mom's song lyrics popped into my head.

*You can do anything.*

*Any time.*

*If you try.*

*See it.*

*Feel it.*

*Be it.*

*Do it.*

*Just try.*

I couldn't magically lift the trunk. I couldn't magically repair the canoe. I couldn't turn back the clock and magically *unsink* the motor boat. But yeah, I could keep trying to fix what was in front of me. Just like what my dad was trying to do when he took me to Bear Island.

"I'm going to start being your father again," he'd said. "After your mother died, I let my depression break apart the relationship I had with you." He put his hand on my shoulder. "I'm going to fix this, but I'll need your help."

For the few weeks before our accident I had my father back. If I hadn't had that time with him and he'd died, I'm not sure how I'd feel about him or how I'd remember him. Yeah, I was extremely sad that my dad was gone, but I was glad that he'd made the effort to be close to me again. I knew that he loved me because of those few weeks we had on Bear Island before the accident.

I wiped a tear from my cheek as the rush of the silty Tanana, mixed in with the wind, filled my ears. The burnt snags swayed a little, and I checked them out. None of the ones closest to me looked as tall as the monster that had fallen, so I was safe for the moment.

But back to the canoe. Mr. Dodge wanted to fix his relationship with Billy but for him to even have that chance, I needed to fix the canoe.

I grabbed the bow and gave it a pull, but it started to bend away from the tree trunk while the rest of the canoe stayed stuck. I stopped pulling, not wanting to make the break worse.

Pressure, I thought. I've got to relieve the pressure.

"Dig," I said. "Dig out the sand below the canoe on the side away from the trunk, and then slide the canoe out."

I grabbed the paddle and dug it into the sand under the bow and pulled some sand out of the way. And then I did it again, thankful that this beach was sandy and not rocky.

*Pressure. You still need to relieve it.*

"Just shut up," I said as I kept digging. I was working the sand out from under the bow of the canoe and along the side of it.

A few minutes later I had about five feet cleared, about a third of the length of the canoe.

"Okay." I set the paddle down, grabbed the bow of the canoe and gave it a pull toward the trench I'd just dug.

The front half of the canoe closest to the trench tilted into it.

But the part of the canoe that was pinned by the trunk tilted upward, and I heard a creak.

The pressure had increased.

"No." I said. "No." I kicked the ground and shook my head. "No."

I felt my eyes getting hot, so I splashed river water on them, but then they started itching from the silt. I untied the bandana, soaked it, rung it out, and retied it around my face. I rubbed my eyes.

*It's not too late. You can still relieve the pressure.*

"But how?" I said.

"How?" I shouted.

I stomped the few steps back to the canoe and studied it. The end of the charred trunk refused to let go of the old canoe.

I squatted and put my shoulder under the trunk and drove my body upward with my legs, but the trunk stayed put, like it'd found its new home and permanently settled in.

Pressure, I thought again.

Pressure.

I couldn't lift the charred snag.

My mind churned away at the problem.

Then I realized that I didn't need to lift it.

I just needed to keep it where it was.

# AT THE CABIN

## [ONE DAY BEFORE THE FIRE]

"My wrist is killing me!" Billy yelled.

I scrambled along the base of the steps. Billy's arm was trapped under his dad's hip.

"Mr. Dodge." I shook his shoulder. "We need you to lift your hip." But I got no response. That's when I noticed the rock next to his head. When he fell, he must've hit it and he was out cold.

I straddled Mr. Dodge and wrapped my arms around his midsection just above his hip.

"I'm going to lift him a little bit," I said to Billy, "and when I do, pull your arm out. Then we can work on getting your dad up the steps." I lifted, and when Billy was free, I unwrapped my arms from around Mr. Dodge.

Billy held his hand toward me. There was a small depression on the top of his wrist and a bulge on the bottom.

"Don't hold it up like that," I said. "It looks like it's broken. You need to support it."

"Billy," Mr. Dodge whispered.

"We're going to get you into the cabin," Billy said. Then he turned to me. "We can deal with my wrist after we take care of my dad. Why'd you have to jump like that? If you—"

"There was a bear coming at me," I cut Billy off. "What was I supposed to do?"

"With three of us on the steps," Billy countered, "that bear would've dodged us if you hadn't leaped sideways and given it an opening."

"You don't know that." I raised my voice. "I just responded faster than you. You would've jumped, too."

"You should've held your ground like I did. You screwed up," Billy said. "I—"

"No, I didn't," I countered. "I just reacted."

"I'm done talking about it for now," Billy said. "We need to deal with my dad." He shook his head. "The boat's gone. And now this."

I stared at Billy for a couple more seconds, not knowing what to say, then I turned to Mr. Dodge. I tapped his shoulder. "We're going to go up the steps but instead of standing up we're going to sit on the steps and scoot up them backwards one step at a time." He turned his head toward me and I sat on the first step and scooted backwards up to the second step. "Just like I'm doing. I'll support your leg."

"I think you're trying to kill me," Mr. Dodge whispered. "You let me fall. Couldn't stand your ground." Mr. Dodged coughed weakly. "My head's killing me and now my leg's bashed up worse too."

My stomach tightened up like it'd just been punched. All I'd done was move when a bear was barreling toward me. It was true that I'd let go of Mr. Dodge. It seemed like the bear was coming right at me. Maybe I had screwed up. Maybe the bear would've gone around all of us if I'd stood my ground. Maybe this was this my fault.

Billy cut into my thoughts. "What can I do to help?" Billy was holding his wrist against his chest.

*Deal with what's most important right now.*

"You can sit next to your dad. And with your good arm," I explained, "you can help him scoot up the steps. It's going to take both of my arms to keep his leg straight." I glanced at the gun on the ground. "Let's do this now," I said, "in case that bear decides to come back."

# CHAPTER 24

## ROCKS.

I needed big rocks. I glanced at the ballast rocks. Too rounded, I thought. I need flat ones.

I walked down the shore until the sand turned to gravel with bigger rocks dotting the land. I gripped a flat rock about as long as a shoebox and several inches thick, picked it up, hugged it to my chest and lugged it back to the canoe. I set it down directly under the tree trunk pinning my canoe to the beach.

My arms turned to rubber carrying big flat rocks up the beach. I built a wide base first. Then I stacked rocks on top of it, and now my pillar was almost touching the bottom of the tree trunk. I didn't know how long I worked on this. The sky grew dimmer and then brighter through the smoke, so I knew I'd spent the *nighttime* hours building the pillar.

Sleepless. My third night on the river.

I'd stopped a couple of times to shove food into my mouth and to drink river water that most of the silt had settled out of, but I was beat and my work was not over yet.

I wedged a small flat rock between the bottom of the trunk and the top of my pillar. I took a step back and studied it.

Pressure.

Could it withstand the pressure?

My head pounded from lack of sleep, but I couldn't rest now. I needed to know if all this rockwork would pay off. The palms of my hands were nicked up from hauling rocks, so when I grabbed the canoe paddle, little stinging sensations, like someone was sticking needles into my palms, peppered my hands.

With the paddle, I dug under the bow of the canoe and hollowed out a space beneath it. Then I worked the paddle under the part of the canoe that was directly below the trunk that pinned it down and gently pushed the sand away. I kept moving more and more sand, hoping the pillar would absorb the pressure I was releasing.

My pile of sand next to the canoe grew to the point where it was going to get in the way when I tried to swing the bow out from under the tree trunk, so I spent some time pushing the sand farther away from the canoe.

I set the paddle down and then stood at the bow of the canoe. I sucked in a big breath through the bandana covering my face and then exhaled. I grabbed the canoe and pulled it toward the river. The canoe slid downward into the space I'd created while the tree trunk stayed put.

The pillar had done its job.

I had done my job.

I pulled the dry bags out of the canoe so it was completely empty and dragged it to a level spot on the beach.

A jagged break in the rim of the canoe stared at me. The ends of the ribs that the rim had held in place poked toward the smoke-filled sky. The rim was actually two narrow pieces of wood screwed together holding the fabric and the end of the ribs between them.

Yeah, I'd done a good job on relieving the pressure.

But now I felt a new pressure. Like a weight was being pressed onto my chest that was crushing my lungs.

My mind kept coming back to Billy and Mr. Dodge back at the cabin, surrounded by a forest fire. Billy using his one good arm to care for his dad and to somehow keep the fire from the cabin.

I tried to strike that image from my mind because it wasn't helping me figure out what I needed to do right now. That was something I had learned on Bear Island, that sometimes you just needed to focus on the present if you wanted to have a future, and if you survived, then later you could obsess over anything you wanted until the next time came where you had to give all your attention to what was in front of you.

I took a deep breath.

I needed to keep moving downriver.

But the one thing I didn't know was the one thing I needed to know. And I needed to know it now.

I stared at the damage like there was a secret that would be revealed if I looked long enough and hard enough.

"The canoe won't work." A bitterness rose from my throat into my mouth and I swallowed it down. "It won't float if I can't fix the break."

# AT THE CABIN

## (ONE DAY BEFORE THE FIRE)

After we got Mr. Dodge to his bunk, I worked a pillow under his head and covered him with a sleeping bag. He said his head was killing him even worse and he closed his eyes and was instantly asleep or passed out. I could see his chest rising and falling so I knew he was still breathing. I made Billy lie down, too, and as he rested, I cleaned up the mess the bear had made of the cabin and looked for things I could use to deal with their injuries, and for the satellite phone so we could try to contact someone for help.

It was like a giant had grabbed the cabin and shaken it up. As I swept loose bits of food and put plates, bowls, and silverware back in their places, my tired mind pounded away with thoughts. All I'd wanted to do was get Mr. Dodge into the cabin so we could care for his injuries, but now, with both he and Billy injured...what could I do to help out?

Out on Bear Island, I had myself to rely on, and if I screwed up, it only affected me. But here, now, I was responsible for everyone's survival. After seeing that the door was cracked open, I wished I had peeked in the window before we'd started hauling Mr. Dodge up the steps.

I wondered what my dad would think of my actions. Safety first, is what he used to always tell me when I'd work with him on building projects.

But when you're in a situation and all you want to do is help, then sometimes you get so focused on helping that you don't see everything. I was so focused on getting Mr. Dodge *safely* up the steps that the open door with a faulty latch, and the squirrel explanation were enough to let me ignore the warning signs.

Safety first.

But what does that mean? By itself, I didn't agree with it. It was too simple.

Survival first.

That's what I thought.

Then Billy's voice jarred me back to the present.

"I'm not going to be much good with this one arm." He was still lying down but was holding his mangled wrist up for me to see.

Billy's hand and wrist had swelled up so it looked like someone had pumped water under his skin. If I hadn't jumped off the steps, he probably wouldn't have a broken wrist.

"We need to splint your wrist." I pointed at some small pieces of wood and an ace bandage. "I found the wood under the cabin while you were asleep. I think it'll do the trick."

Billy glanced at his wrist. "Have you ever put a splint on anything?"

"No," I said. "But I can do it. Just rest your arm on the pillows." The wood was thin and light but when I put a piece against Billy's wrist he winced and pulled away.

*Soft but stable. Just keep that wrist from moving. That's all.*

I looked Billy in the eye. "I think I've got a better idea."

"I hope so," Billy said.

"Let's try this." I pointed to the sleeping pad on his bunk. "It's soft but also firm. I can cut a piece, wrap it around your forearm and use the ace bandage to keep it there."

With a knife I cut a piece of the pad, fitted it around Billy's arm from just below his elbow to half way up his hand and then wrapped the ace bandage around it—a perfect splint.

Then Mr. Dodge let out a soft moan.

"Dad," Billy said, taking a step toward him.

"Billy," Mr. Dodge said, staring up at him. Then his eyes shifted toward me. "Tom," he said. Then he moved his other leg and howled out in pain.

# CHAPTER 25

**I HAD TO** try something. Anything. I stared at the ribs poking up into the air.

Bones, I thought.

Ribs are like bones. The fabric is the skin. All the pieces of wood are the bones. The rim is the broken piece—the broken bone. How do you put together a broken bone?

I pictured Billy's dangling wrist and Mr. Dodge's broken leg.

And then I had an idea.

"Splint," I said. "I need to splint the rim of the canoe."

Somehow. With something.

A crooked line cut through the rim where it'd broken. A couple of the screws holding the two pieces of wood together had been ripped free from the impact. And that had caused four of the ribs to detach from the rim and lose their curve. The fabric was undamaged, but without the curved ribs to keep it bent outward, the skin on the front left of the canoe under the break was straight, and stuck up higher than the broken rim, just like the ribs.

As long as the fabric didn't collapse, I thought it would be okay. I mean, I didn't care how it looked, I just needed to fix the boat so it would keep floating.

I pushed on the bow of the canoe and felt the left-side start to buckle. I thought about paddling and sometimes having to turn the canoe crosswise to the current and worried that the force of the river would buckle the canoe and water would pour in if I didn't make a strong splint.

Upriver, on the top of the island, I knew there'd be a cache of driftwood.

I walked the shore. Every spruce tree was burnt up. The understory was ash.

At the end of the small island a pile of driftwood—trees, logs and branches that had traveled the current and then become stuck—was perched, waiting for the next big rise in the river to carry it all downstream. A couple hundred muddy feet separated the partially unburnt pile of driftwood from the completely burnt forest.

The wind was blowing stronger at the tip of the island, and little waves were washing against the shore.

Pick some pieces and get back to the canoe, I thought. I glanced back at the canoe. It was still sitting there broken and battered, but undisturbed.

I searched the edge of the pile for the right sized pieces and settled for two bleached out branches still attached to a big log that was lodged into the beach. Each was about as big around as my wrist. I broke them off, and then using my foot for leverage, broke them each again to get them more in line with the two-to-three foot length I wanted.

Back at the canoe, I held the two pieces of wood on either side of the rim, centering the break, and pushed them together. The tops of the ribs were still poking out above the rim, and the fabric was still straight, not curved like the it was on the rest of the canoe, but I didn't think any of that would matter. The two pieces of broken rim were squashed back together, the two screws re-entering their stripped-out holes.

What would matter was being able to prevent the canoe from buckling. And this splint would do that. At least that's what I hoped.

I released the pressure, and the screws popped back out of their holes. I set the splint pieces down.

"This will work," I said. "It has to work."

But the rim of a canoe wasn't like a broken knee or a broken wrist where you could place a splint and then wrap tape or ace bandages all the way around it and the broken limb.

The rim of the canoe was attached to the rest of the canoe, and I couldn't wrap something around the whole canoe to hold the splint in place.

I opened the food bag and ate a granola bar. I took a drink from my water bottle. Then I dug the pot out and filled it with river water and let it set because I knew that figuring out how to actually splint the boat would take some time.

I found my pocketknife, pulled the blade out, and cut a hunk of cheese. I opened the box of crackers and ate some of them with the cheese. I hadn't realized how hungry I was until now. I picked up the knife and cut another piece of cheese.

I wiped the blade on my pants and was about to close my knife back up, but then I paused, staring at the tip. I touched it with my finger. It was sharp.

I glanced at the canoe and then back at my knife.

Canoe.

Knife.

And now I knew how to make the splint work.

# AT THE CABIN

## [ONE DAY BEFORE THE FIRE]

"Mr. Dodge," I said. "We've got to splint your leg so you don't damage it when you move around."

"It's killing me," Mr. Dodge said in a weak voice. He looked over to Billy and then back to me. "I wish your uncle would've just taken you already. I. . ." Then his eyes closed and his voice trailed off.

Uncle Jim, I thought. He wasn't expecting us to be back for another month at least. And, as much as I dreaded the thought of leaving Alaska to go live with him in Michigan, it was the least of my worries at the moment.

I turned to Billy. "We've got to find that satellite phone. Now."

Mr. Dodge groaned. "The phone's gone," he whispered. "It was in the boat."

My stomach clenched up. No boat. No phone.

"Dad," Billy said, "do you have a spare?"

"No," Mr. Dodge whispered. "You boys gotta get me out of here." He clutched his head.

After we worked Mr. Dodge's soaked pants off, we discovered that the lower half of his leg was black and blue, and swollen. He cried out in pain when we pulled a loose-fitting pair of sweatpants onto him.

"My whole leg hurts." Mr. Dodge opened his eyes. "From just above the knee all the way down." He looked me in the eye. "And my head's killing me, thanks to you."

"Mr. Dodge," I said. "Right now, we just need to get your leg fixed up. I'll splint it like Billy's, plus I'll add some wood for support." I pointed at Billy and he held up his arm, splinted with the sleeping pad. "Your lower leg looks like it's the worst part. But if you're hurting above the knee too, I'll splint the whole thing."

Mr. Dodge stared at me. I couldn't tell if he was understanding what I was saying or if he was about to pass out again, or just plain angry, but then he nodded and said, "Do it."

Mr. Dodge shifted his leg and screamed again.

"Try to stay still," I said.

I cut a long section of the sleeping pad with the knife and placed it next to Mr. Dodge's leg. It ran from his ankle to just below his hip. "We'll need two thin boards about this long." I grabbed the piece of cut sleeping pad and held it up.

"Under the cabin," Mr. Dodge whispered. "That's where Buck stores his spare building supplies."

"And, we'll need some rope or sheets or something to tie the wood and the sleeping pad to your leg," I added.

"There's rope in the shed." Billy bounced on his toes. "Even with one arm, I can get it." Billy ran out the door to get the rope, leaving me and Mr. Dodge.

Mr. Dodge took a big breath and then exhaled, his belly moving up and then down. "Tom," Mr. Dodge whispered, "There's some things I need to tell Billy. It's about his mother. I—"

Right then Billy burst in the door, a rope dangling from his good hand. "I know how we can get out of here. Buck's old canoe. The three of us can take it down the river." Billy smiled.

I felt a chill travel up my spine. My heart thumped through my shirt. Images of me and my dad flipping our kayak and being pummeled by giant waves filled my brain.

No way was I going to get into that old canoe.

# CHAPTER 26

**I DUNKED** my bandana in the river, rung it out and retied it around my face. Then, with my knife in hand, approached the canoe.

The number one thing I'd been stressed about when I set out downriver was the canoe fabric. Could I keep it from getting torn up from contact with sharp rocks and logs? The big tear toward the back of the canoe had shown me just how thin the fabric was that separated me from death by drowning.

And now here I was, about to intentionally punch a bunch of holes in the fabric.

Part of me thought I might be acting too quickly, like maybe there was a better way, a safer way, but I didn't have time to slowly think up every way to solve this problem. I needed a solution. Somehow my brain had come up with one, but now that I was actually about to follow through, I was hesitating.

Some of my mom's song lyrics popped into my brain.

> *You have to change.*
> *Change. Change. Change.*
> *Your actions might look strange.*
> *Strange. Strange. Strange.*
> *But if you understand,*
> *Then you'll make the change.*
> *And rearrange.*
> *Others might not understand.*

*Even you might doubt your plan.*
*Don't be afraid to take a stand.*

Her song was more about someone making a change and not being afraid of what other people would think. But the way I saw it, the song could apply to my situation, too. Putting a bunch of holes in a canoe I was going to paddle did seem strange, but I needed to make this change now.

I grabbed one of the splint-pieces and held it up to the broken rim to measure one last time.

Make as few holes as possible, I thought. And make them just big enough so you can thread a piece of rope through them.

I set the splint down and gripped the rim of the canoe. Then, I pressed the tip of my knife into the fabric about a half-inch below the rim and twisted it back and forth.

The tip poked through, creating a tiny hole, and I kept twisting, pushing more of the knife into the hole until an inch of the knife poked through.

I pulled the knife out and picked up my rope. The end was frayed, so I cut it off and poked the freshly trimmed end through the hole.

"Easy," I said. "It went through easy."

I made five more holes in the fabric, trying to evenly space them along the part of the rim I planned on splinting.

Canoe First Aid.

The wind started blowing again, and I looked up at the charred trees swaying.

"Just keep working," I said. "Keep working."

I heard a pop.

And then a crack.

The beach vibrated as another snag hit the ground—this one a good hundred-feet from me.

I picked up the rope that I'd been using as my stern rope.

In the end I decided to cut six small pieces of rope instead of using one longer piece, figuring if one knot failed there'd still be five more holding the splint. I'd used about twelve feet of my stern rope and estimated I still had about twenty feet left.

I threaded each of the six short lengths of rope through their holes, then I grabbed the two pieces of splint-wood and positioned them in place. Every time I tried to tie one of the ropes around the splint I'd have to loosen my grip, and that would cause the rim wood to separate.

*Tie a few of them loosely. Just to hold the splint in place. And then tie the others tightly. And then go back and tighten the loose ones.*

"Okay, okay, okay," I said, knowing my dad was right. He hadn't told me to make a splint in the first place, but now that I'd done all the thinking and all the work, suddenly he'd reappeared as a know-it-all.

It wasn't a pretty job, but at least it seemed to be holding the rim in place. I didn't know how the canoe would respond in the water with the added weight of the splint, and with the change in shape of the fabric, but I'd find out soon enough.

I lifted the bow of the canoe, swung it toward the river and set it down so it was just touching the water. Then I did the same thing with the stern.

I reloaded the bow with all the dry bags except for the two yellow ones.

Variables.

I'd changed four things.

I'd moved myself to the middle.

I'd added a patch to the back.

I'd added a splint to the front.

I'd eliminated the ballast rocks.

I sure hoped this boat wouldn't require much more repair because I was running out of spots to fix.

Close to a hundred and fifty miles to go, I thought.

I hoped the smoke would clear.

I hoped I'd run into someone long before I got to the takeout spot.

I hoped Billy and his dad were doing okay.

But mostly, I hoped this old battered canoe would stay afloat so I wouldn't drown in the cold silty waters of the Tanana River.

"Enough, thinking," I said. "Enough." I just needed to paddle away from these charred islands and see how the canoe responds.

I lifted the bow into the water and set it down. Then I lifted the stern and walked the rest of the canoe into the river. As the current started tugging on it, I hopped in, stepped over the strut in the middle of the canoe and settled into my new position in the center of the boat.

I glanced back at the patch on the right. Then glanced forward to the splint on the left. I dug my paddle in and pulled. Then I did it again.

The canoe had a wobble to it that was new, and it leaned a little to the left, but the patch in the back was riding above the water line and the front of the canoe wasn't buckling.

I cleared the lower end of the charred islands, and the water stretched out from one smoke obscured bank to the other. The river was making an enormous bend to the left.

Stay in the middle, I thought.

The Tanana was so much bigger than the Olsen. The Olsen was an earth worm and the Tanana a giant python.

As I rounded the bend, I saw a thin red line on the horizon. It appeared to reach from bank to bank.

I squinted.

Flames spanning the river?

I dug my paddle in and pulled.

Whatever was ahead, I needed to paddle through it.

# AT THE CABIN

## [ONE DAY BEFORE THE FIRE]

Billy and I studied the canoe in the shed. Its off-white fabric covered with the waterproofing sealant we'd finished putting on just before we hiked to the forks. The thin wooden ribs, some of them repaired with duct tape and tied together with twine. The cracked knobby wood that made up the struts.

I ran my hand along the fabric that made up the shell of the canoe. A sharp stick or a jagged rock could do some damage.

Real quick.

Water would pour in and it'd sink.

And we'd be swimming.

Or trying to.

Mr. Dodge with his hurt leg and head injury.

Billy with his broken wrist.

Most people traveling long distances on rivers used motorboats or sturdy canoes or kayaks. Not something made of sticks and cloth.

There had to be another way.

Billy lifted one end of the canoe with his good arm and then set it down. "It's lighter than I thought it'd be."

I grabbed the other end and lifted it and then put it back down. "It'll be a lot heavier when we're all in it."

"It's way too small for all three of us," Billy said.

My throat was dry and constricted. I swallowed, but still felt like it was closing up.

"I can't leave my dad here all alone," Billy continued. "You know that, right?"

I rocked the canoe back and forth. Then I ran my hand

along the bumpy, thin fabric again. The kayak me and my dad had paddled was massive compared to this, and in the end, it hadn't mattered. It'd been smashed to bits and I'd barely made it to shore. And even though my dad's voice told me that the accident wasn't my fault, sometimes I still felt like it was, like if I'd done one thing differently maybe we wouldn't have had the accident, maybe I wouldn't have caused his death.

And now, with Mr. Dodge, I was the one that had caused his head injury. Maybe I'd made his leg worse when he fell, too. I didn't know. What I did know was that I didn't want to be responsible for another person dying, especially my best friend's father.

But I was terrified of the thought of paddling this beat-up canoe two hundred miles through the wilderness.

Alone.

I hadn't even wanted to paddle this old death-trap-of-a-canoe in front of the cabin with Billy. My whole body was trembling.

"No way," I said. I raised my voice. "I can't do this. I'd never make it. There's got to be another way." Then I turned and walked out of the shed.

# CHAPTER 27

**I LET** the canoe ride with the current, putting my paddle in the water and flaring it when I started to drift off from the center.

I was in what seemed like the middle of the bend now, and my brain was registering my mistake, making sense of the illusion of flames on the water.

The smoke made everything difficult to see, but now I could make out the river jogging to the right just beyond the big left bend, which I was in the middle of.

And yeah, the forest was actively burning on both sides. The zigzagging of the river combined with the smoke made it look like the flames were continuous. But really it was two flaming points of land on opposite sides of the river.

"Good," I said, when I realized I didn't have to paddle a flammable boat through a wall of fire. And then I thought, this must be pretty bad because I'm relieved that I'm only surrounded by fire and not in it.

Perspective, I thought. My perspective is like this: Okay, I can survive right now because I am not going to get burned up. I glanced at the splint and then looked over my shoulder at the patch. The boat is still floating, that's a good thing.

A gust of wind hit me from the left and pushed the bow of the boat to the right, so I dug my paddle in on the right side of the boat and pulled and the boat turned back to the center.

One paddle stroke, I thought. One paddle stroke and I'm back on course.

Leverage, I thought. I've got more leverage sitting in the middle.

If I had been in the stern, it would have taken three or four strokes to do what I'd just done.

I had to reach farther to find the water since the middle of the boat was wider than the stern, but the positive effect of the paddling from the middle more than made up for it.

Splash.

Plunk.

On the left bank of the river, flaming trees—trees that would've turned into sweepers—were dropping into the water.

Splash.

That one had come from the right.

Another gust of wind hit me. I flared my paddle to keep the canoe pointed downriver.

Ash was now in the air, so I pulled my hat lower on my head. I kept paddling as gray-white flakes coated everything in my canoe.

Somewhere downriver, this fire had to end. But really, for all I knew, the forest was burning up all the way to the bridge where I was planning on taking out and beyond. I guessed the bridge was still over a hundred miles away. Could a fire be that big? Yes, I told myself, yes, it could.

I noticed small pockets of land where birches grew that weren't actively burning, even though the spruce was on fire all around them. I didn't know why the birches weren't burning as easily as the spruce. Maybe they had more moisture in them. Truth was, I just didn't know, but it was obvious from what I was seeing that it was probably true.

The more birch the better, I thought. Paddle until you find a whole birch forest without spruce, if one exists around here.

The only way I'd survived on Bear Island was continuing to choose to try, no matter what obstacle I found in front of myself.

Had I wanted to quit while I was stranded on Bear Island? Yeah, like three hundred times a day, I'd wished I didn't have to do what I'd needed to do. But the alternative was to choose death. And I didn't want to die.

And Billy wasn't a quitter either. When I was staying with him, after his dad shattered a dish and stormed out of the house in anger, Billy waited up for him in the kitchen.

"My dad's come a long way but he's still got a ways to go." Billy lowered his voice. "I think my mom may have given up on him. I can't blame her.

know what it's like be on the receiving end of his anger."

It was almost midnight and my eyes wanted to close. "What are you going to do if he comes home angrier than when he left?" I was sitting here because I'd noticed that Mr. Dodge was more likely to restrain himself if more than just family were around.

"I'm going to remind him of how he beat his drinking problem, and if he keeps trying, he can beat his anger problem too." Billy tapped his fingers on the table. "But he's got to know I'm rooting for him, especially if my mom isn't."

"Sometimes people only change when they're ready," I said. "Like my dad. I don't know why or how he climbed out of his depression, but he did."

"I get that," Billy said. "But I think sometimes people don't know they're ready to change until someone shows them they are." Billy cracked a small smile. "If I can somehow help my dad out of his anger, maybe my mom will get on board too."

I doubled down on my paddling. The sooner I got to where I was going, the greater the chance that time wouldn't run out on Billy and his dad. And, if in my heart I knew I had given it my all and they still died, then maybe I could live with myself. Maybe. But it wouldn't be easy. Those deaths would tear at me every day.

A jolt from below pitched me forward, and I hit the strut separating me from the pile of gear in the bow of the canoe. I popped back up on my knees.

The bottom?

Had I hit the bottom?

My canoe was still floating but had turned sharply to the right.

I dug my paddle in and pulled and flared it out to turn it back to the center, but the response was sluggish. Like the current had slowed way down.

Or the canoe had gotten heavy.

Or something was pulling on it.

I paddled again, flared my paddle again, but got the same response. The canoe drifting sluggishly to the right.

Then I saw the water running under my left knee.

Water, in the canoe.

Something off to the left caught my eye so I turned, and there, bobbing in the current, was a charred log.

It flared out from the bow at a forty-five-degree angle.

I reached with my paddle toward the log. I had to disconnect it from the canoe. Now water was running under both my knees.

I was about to try to push the log away with my paddle and then I stopped.

Impaled, my mind screamed.

Somewhere under that pile of dry bags, part of that log must've poked through the fabric and now I was taking on water. And it must still be hanging on or else my paddling would have freed the canoe.

But if I pushed off from the log, then there'd be nothing plugging the hole.

The water would pour in faster.

I had to make it to shore.

With the log attached.

I scanned both shores for birches. I needed a safe spot in the burning spruce, and I needed it now. If the canoe sunk in the middle of the river, I'd sink, too.

# AT THE CABIN

## [ONE DAY BEFORE THE FIRE]

"Tom, you have to go in the canoe." Billy looked toward his dad, sleeping on the bunk, his leg splinted with wood, a sleeping pad, and tied with rope. "He needs a doctor."

"But—"

"No one is going to come looking for us," Billy interrupted. "We're supposed to be gone for another month. You know that. What is your problem?"

"It's the canoe," I paused, "you know it's a ragged old boat. You saw what it's made of. I don't trust it. It'll be poked full of holes in no time."

Billy clenched his teeth. "You haven't even been in it yet."

"I don't trust myself, either," I continued. "I've never paddled a boat on a fast-moving river and now I'm supposed to do it all by myself in that old deathtrap?" I shook my head. "I'll walk out. That way, I'll be more likely to actually make it."

"It'll take too long," Billy countered. "The river is windy. There's miles of thick brush. You'd have to walk around every bend, or risk getting lost trying to take short cuts."

Mr. Dodge let out a groan from the bed, and Billy went over and stood by him.

Billy had his hand on his dad's arm. "Dad. You're gonna be okay." Billy looked over at me. "We're going to get some help." He raised his voice. "Tom's going to take the canoe."

Billy kept staring at me, like he was waiting for me to say something, but my throat was so tight I couldn't say anything. He turned back toward his dad.

Mr. Dodge groaned again.

Billy faced me again and looked me dead in the eye.

"I can take care of my dad with one arm for now. But if he gets sicker, or if his head injury is serious, he needs a doctor like yesterday. You've got to go soon. You need to get ready now."

"You know that canoe is a piece of junk," I countered. "You want to send me on a death trip?" I paused. "If your dad hadn't run us off and then sunk the boat, he wouldn't have broken his leg or hit his head. Period."

"What if it were your dad who had the head injury?" Billy asked. "And you knew taking that old canoe was the only sure way to get some help. What would you do? Let him die because you're scared?" Billy lowered his voice to a whisper. "My dad may not be perfect, but he's the only one I've got. I haven't stuck with him all this time to just give up on him now."

I took a breath. Truth was, I would've done *anything* to save my dad. "I'll do it. I'll take the canoe, but there's no guarantee I'll make it in that thing."

"Just make sure you're wearing your life vest at all times," Billy said. "It'll keep you from sinking if you have an accident."

"I know," I said softly, swallowing the vomit that was in the back of my throat. My life vest would be the most important piece of equipment I had.

# CHAPTER 28

**SILTY** water covered my kneecaps and pushed on my thighs as I paddled toward the right bank with no islands in sight to land on.

My breath came and went in short gasps. If I didn't make it to shore the silty water and strong current would drag me under.

The charred log bobbed next to the canoe. It was like a leech had attached itself to the canoe and wasn't going to let go.

On the shore, I could see individual spruce trees burning.

Up ahead, a few birch trees swayed in the smoke. The spruce trees around them were charred snags, having already burned up, and back from the bank I could see a red glow, like the fire was marching across the land. Downriver, trees burned on the bank and yellow-orange flames reached skyward.

I kept digging my paddle in, aiming for the birches. The tiny spot of shore the grove of birch trees guarded was made up of mud and gravel.

The log must've bottomed out first because in an instant the stern swung out and the side of the canoe sat snug against the log it was impaled on, and I was facing upriver instead of down like I was a second ago.

The canoe wasn't going anywhere, but there was no way I could even try to fix it unless I got it to shore.

I leaned forward and grabbed the bow rope and wrapped it around my wrist.

Then I thought, the gear. In case the boat sunk, I needed to get the gear ashore now.

I dropped the bow rope and threw the two yellow dry bags on shore.

Then, I quickly untied the dry bags in the bow and threw them onshore, thankful that they all landed on the ground and not in the water.

I stuck my hand into the water pooled in the bow of the canoe. The end of a sharp branch grazed my palm. On either side of the branch, I felt a jagged tear in the thin gray padding and under that, loose fabric flapping, like that branch had punched through and then had moved back and forth, widening the hole.

The end of the branch had poked through between two of the five pieces of wood that ran lengthwise, making up the floor of the canoe. Somehow it had stayed stuck even though the hole seemed way bigger than the end of the branch.

My hands were going numb from keeping them under water.

*Get out of the boat.*

I grabbed the bow rope again and looked across the ten or twelve feet of river that separated me from the shore. I didn't know how deep it was.

The other rope, I thought. I might need the other rope to lengthen the stern rope. I fished around in the silty water in the bow and found the rope I'd used to tie in the dry bags. I crawled to the stern of the canoe and tied the rope to the stern rope to give it more length.

Somehow, I needed to get the canoe off this log. Maybe from shore I could pull on the stern and work the canoe off. Or maybe pull from the bow. If I could pull the canoe upward, I'd be able to free it.

No way could I lift the canoe up while I was in it.

My only chance was getting on shore and trying to figure it out from there.

With the bow rope in one hand and the stern rope in the other, I slowly stood up in the center of the canoe.

Then I bent my knees and leaped toward shore.

# AT THE CABIN

## [ONE DAY BEFORE THE FIRE]

"There are no life vests," Mr. Dodge said in a weak voice.

I felt my stomach go raw. "What! No way! I'm not going without a life vest."

"Let me explain," Mr. Dodge whispered. "I had all three vests with me when I went upriver, so you'd be safe when we came back together." Mr. Dodge shifted his leg and winced in pain. He was sitting on his bunk with his back against the wall, and his splinted leg was propped up by some folded blankets and a pillow. "When I got the boat stuck on the sweeper and it started to sink, I threw the gun to shore, but lost everything else. I didn't even have time to put my life vest on." Mr. Dodge closed his eyes.

The vest I'd brought on this trip was my dad's—it was the only thing of his I'd found washed up on shore after the accident on Bear Island.

I turned to Billy and said, "We're going to have to come up with a different plan." Then I walked outside and slammed the door behind me.

My eyes were on fire as I felt a few tears escape. I wanted my dad's life vest back and I wanted it now. It was something I thought I'd always have. The thing that most reminded me of who he was and what he loved to do. Plus, every time I'd imagined the canoe flipping, I'd seen myself wearing that life vest as I tried to make it shore so I wouldn't be dragged underwater. And, my survival kit was gone because it had been in the pocket of the vest.

I looked at the canoe sitting in front of the cabin. Me and Billy had taken it out of the shed so I could figure out what to take and how to pack it.

Even though I thought it was cool that someone could make a boat out of basically nothing, the idea of using the boat for a long journey all by myself, especially without a life vest, made me want to crawl under a rock and hide.

Billy stepped outside and closed the door. "So, you're going back on your word?" He shook his head. "I thought I knew you better."

"You even said it yourself," I countered, "*just wear your life vest. I—*"

"That was when I thought you'd have one." Billy pointed toward the window. "You want my dad to die? You want to sit here and watch him die?"

"I don't want anyone to die," I replied. "Including myself."

"I'll go." Billy raised his splinted arm. "Even with one arm, I'll take my chances. But you'll need to take care of my dad."

"Wait, I—"

"And he better not die," Billy interrupted. "Just because he's not as nice as your dad was, doesn't mean he deserves less of a chance to make it."

I raised my voice. "Just because you have a dad and I don't doesn't mean you get to make all the decisions."

"You are so selfish," Billy yelled. "I've never seen you act so selfish."

"If selfish means not wanting to die," I shouted back, "then yeah, I'm selfish."

"We're not through with this yet, but right now my dad needs me." Then Billy walked back into the cabin and slammed the door.

I glanced at the canoe. It was a deathtrap, especially without a life vest. But it'd be even more of a death trap for a person with only one good arm.

# CHAPTER 29

## (BILLY AND HIS DAD)

**"IT MAY** not always look like it, but I'm trying to do better," my dad whispered. His forehead was sweaty and his eyes were closed. "Billy. There's so much I'm sorry for." My dad opened his eyes. "If I could make it all up to you I would. What's done is done. But I'll keep on trying whether I live for a few more hours or till I'm a hundred and ten."

"Dad." I put my hand on his arm. "I hear you."

A single tear rolled down his cheek, and I wiped it away. Then he closed his eyes. I knew he was in a lot of pain, but he'd stopped complaining about it. He seemed stable but could only manage a few words at a time.

I hadn't brought up what he'd said about me just saving myself and letting him die. I just hoped he'd come to his senses if worse came to worst. And, I didn't want to argue with him about something that might not even happen. I mean, Tom may have already gotten word to someone and help could be on the way.

The air inside the cabin was hot and stuffy. I was wearing shorts and a T-shirt and I was still sweating like crazy. I'd made a couple of trips to the river, peering at the sky, trying to see through the thick yellow smoke, searching for flames.

I'd rummaged through the shed where Buck had stored his canoe and had crawled under the cabin searching for anything that would help me and my dad survive a fire if it started eating through the woods around the cabin, and had piled up the items onto the porch, ready to act.

I stood up and walked to the cabin door. "Dad," I said, "I'm going to check the sky."

He nodded, keeping his eyes closed.

I opened the door and put my hand over my mouth. Even though the air inside the cabin was bad, it was way worse outside. I wondered how Tom was dealing with just plain old breathing. I walked the trail to the river. A hot dry wind blew from downriver, and on the horizon I spotted a red glow, like the sun was setting except it was the middle of the afternoon. I ran back to the cabin. It was time to put my plan into action to try to save me and my dad.

# CHAPTER 30

**I LANDED** in waist deep water and fell forward. I squeezed my eyes closed as my face hit the river, not wanting them to fill with silt. With my hands, I pushed myself up. Water poured off me. I still had the bow rope in one hand, but the stern rope was floating free somewhere.

The bottom of the river rose steeply, and the current tugged at me as I waded toward dry land.

On shore, I turned and looked at the canoe. The stern had swung farther away from shore. Somehow when I had jumped the canoe shifted, but the bow was still held fast by the log.

I pulled in the slack on the bowline and tugged on it, which made the canoe shake but did nothing to free it. I walked upriver a few steps, continuing to yank on the rope, until I was even with the bow. That increased my rope length to about fifteen feet on shore, but it still wasn't enough to reach the trees to tie off the boat.

I stared at the water under the bow and then toward shore, trying to imagine where the log had grounded out.

"I need to free the boat," I said. Then I shivered and realized that I was soaking wet and the wind was starting to blow. The dry bags lay scattered on the small beach. I reached for my clothing bag, and then stopped.

"No," I said. "Not yet." Because I knew I'd just get all wet again. I didn't know how I was going to free the canoe, but after tugging on the rope and getting nowhere, I knew I needed to go back into the river and try.

Down the shore I could see flames eating their way through a patch of spruce. The birches I was holed up in dominated the riverbank for about thirty feet.

A tiny window of protection. A birch window in a wall of spruce. Even though I wasn't sure if the birches would protect me, I knew it was way better than being in the spruce.

One thing, I thought. It's one thing that I did right. Landing the canoe by the birches.

A shiver ran through my body as I refocused on the canoe.

Lift it.

I needed to lift it off the log it was snagged on. Now that I was out of the canoe it'd be easier to lift. I remembered how light it had been when Billy and I had first carried it out of the shed and down to the river.

And now I wished that once I'd thrown all the gear ashore, I had just eased myself into the water over the edge of the canoe and had tried to free it up.

I tugged on the rope again.

The canoe didn't even budge.

The log was firmly anchoring it.

But also, the canoe looked different. Smaller.

And then I knew.

Less of the canoe was above the water line.

It must be filling with water.

"No!" I screamed.

I dropped the rope, ran to the gray dry bag, opened it up and dumped it.

I grabbed the pot and started toward the canoe because I knew that that canoe was my best chance at surviving. It was Billy's best chance. It was Mr. Dodge's best chance.

Before I re-entered the river, I tugged my boots off, remembering how I had almost drowned out on Bear Island when they'd filled with water and dragged me down.

With sopping wet socks clinging to my feet, I ripped the bandana off my face, stuffed it into my hat, tossed my hat so it lay next to the gray dry bag.

I took in a smoky breath and coughed. I stared at the sinking canoe. Then out of the corner my eye I caught a glimpse of yellow and turned.

The bark on one of the birch trees protecting this beach had burst into flames.

Without a life vest, I was trapped between the river and fire.

My heart thumped through my soaked clothing and my teeth chattered as I walked into the river.

# AT THE CABIN

## [ONE DAY BEFORE THE FIRE]

"Watch out for the bear," Mr. Dodge mumbled. "Here it comes."

I walked over to his bunk and shook his arm. "You were dreaming."

Mr. Dodge opened his eyes. "Tom," he said softly. "I know I haven't always been there for Billy."

I nodded.

He pointed at Billy. "There's things I need to tell him. I know I can own up to what I did wrong, how I wasn't always around, and how I treated him sometimes." Mr. Dodge gripped his head with his hands and winced. Then he looked me in the eye and whispered, "I want a chance to make it right back home. And that, Tom, is going to depend on you getting some help so I don't die out here."

I swallowed. "I know."

Mr. Dodge let out a breath and then closed his eyes.

I looked over at Billy getting some much-needed sleep after our argument.

Before my uncle arrived from Michigan, Billy had convinced his parents to let me live with them, keeping me out of a foster home. He'd always had my back.

In third grade when this big kid, Matt, was pushing me against the fence on the playground, I was paralyzed with fear. Billy had jumped between us and told Matt to leave me alone. Matt ended up punching Billy instead of me. And even after he got punched, Billy still wouldn't let Matt near me. That took guts and loyalty.

I went back outside and hauled the canoe and the gear down to the water. If I was going to do this, I needed to get started.

I turned and faced the cabin and saw Billy coming down the trail carrying the one and only cracked and decaying paddle we'd found in the shed.

"I knew you'd come through," Billy said.

"Don't say too much," I countered. "Or I might change my mind again."

"You mean you might back out again?" Billy shook his head. "I'll go instead."

"Just shut up and help me pack." Truth was, I was still angry about Billy blaming me for jumping out of the way when the bear charged and for trying to force me to go. He hadn't apologized for what he'd said and neither had I. For all I knew, he was still angry, too. Usually we could laugh and joke around even when we were doing something serious. I wondered if we'd ever be able to be like that again.

Billy held the canoe in the water while I put the dry bags in and tied them with a loose rope. I put the final bag in the stern of the canoe and straddled it, kneeling. It felt like the best way to paddle, but my knees were already aching from being on the bumpy wood frame. "My knees," I said to Billy. "This isn't going to work."

"That sleeping pad you cut up to make this splint," Billy held his wrist up, "just cut a couple of pieces for knee pads." He shook his head. "Then you need to go."

I climbed out of the canoe. "Are you okay holding the boat while I get the sleeping pad?"

Billy nodded. "No problem. Just go do it before I take the canoe and leave you here. My dad's injuries can't wait any longer."

I ran up the trail to the cabin and opened the door, and what I saw made me stop in my tracks.

# CHAPTER 31

**THE COLD** silty water pressed on my legs and then my stomach and then my chest. My feet fell away from the bottom and my head went under once before I finally gripped the bow of the canoe in my free hand with the river running just below my chin. The current was trying to pull me downriver and it would have if I didn't have the boat to hang on to.

I tossed the pot into the canoe. Then, with both hands, I pulled myself up and spied the paddle, one of my water bottles and my kneepads floating in the water-filled canoe.

My feet found the log that grounded out the canoe. There must be a branch protruding from the log that had impaled the canoe.

If I could break that branch, I could free the canoe. With one hand on the rim of the canoe, I ran my other hand under the water and along the fabric but felt nothing. I scooted around the bow so I was on the side facing the expanse of river and explored some more with my free hand but again felt nothing.

Feet, I thought. I'll use my feet. With both hands on the rim of the canoe just forward from where I'd repaired it, I extended my arms and ran my feet along the underside of the canoe.

Bump.

I tried to figure out how big the branch was by using the balls of my feet to explore it.

Too big.

Too large to break, I realized, as my feet scoured over a branch that seemed to be as big around as a coffee can.

A shiver rocked my body. Maybe the end of it was jagged, or maybe a smaller branch that had grown off the branch my feet had explored had punctured the canoe.

It didn't matter. I couldn't break the big branch. Now my only chance was to bail out the canoe, hop back into the water and try to rock it free after it was light and empty.

*Go in right over the tip. Equal weight on each side. Otherwise you'll capsize.*

I moved to the tip of the bow, put my palms on the rim of the canoe, and pushed myself upward until my belly was pressing against the very front of the canoe. Then I leaned forward and reached for the closest strut running crosswise on the canoe. I latched onto it and pulled myself over the bow.

I rolled into the cold bath of silty water in the canoe and knelt.

At least one foot of water covered the bottom of the canoe. The patch in the back right of the canoe was totally submerged and I could see water bubbling in that area so water was coming in through that hole, too. I grabbed the pot by the handle, dunked it into the water filling the canoe, and then poured it over the edge.

Dunk.

Pour.

I kept doing this in a frenzy. I couldn't lose this boat. Even though I was soaked, the constant movement from bailing out the canoe warmed me up. Or, at least it prevented me from feeling colder.

I was scraping along the floor of the canoe now, only filling the pot up halfway before dumping it.

"Okay," I said. "Okay."

I glanced toward shore and saw my collection of dry bags scattered on the small beach. The one birch tree that had caught fire was still burning but the others hadn't caught yet.

I needed to get the canoe to the beach. I'd hoped that just getting the water out of the boat would raise it and let it float free, but I could see the end of the branch poking through, holding the canoe hostage. Water bubbled through the hole it had created.

I couldn't let the canoe refill with water. Kneeling in the middle of the canoe, I extended my arms out to my sides and grabbed the canoe and gently rocked it side-to-side.

"No, deal," I said, as I watched the canoe stay seated on the log.

My weight, I thought. It's keeping the canoe pinned.

I bailed a few more pots of water, and then rocked the canoe again. No luck.

*You need to do something different.*

"Shut up," I said. "Just shut up." But I knew my dad was right.

I looked down at the silty water flowing by my stranded canoe.

I had one thing to try. One thing my dad was driving at. One thing that I didn't want to do. One thing that I was terrified of doing, especially without a life vest.

But if I didn't do it, I may as well kiss the canoe goodbye.

Even if I did do it, there was no guarantee that it would work.

An image of Billy and his dad surrounded by flames flashed into my mind.

Water was flowing through the hole faster now, like maybe rocking the canoe back and forth had widened the hole. And soon the back patch would be riding low enough that water would start pouring through it again.

I glanced toward shore and saw that another birch tree had caught on fire. At least my gear was right at the shoreline but when I did get the canoe ashore I'd have to keep a careful watch on the fire as I figured out what to do to fix the canoe.

I shivered once. I was cooling down fast now that I wasn't bailing. The wind hitting my soaked clothing was sucking the heat out of my body.

And what I needed to do next would just make me colder and colder.

# AT THE CABIN
## [ONE DAY BEFORE THE FIRE]

Mr. Dodge was propped up on his bunk with his legs straight out, his back leaning against the wall. His eyes were closed and his head was tilted to one side.

And resting just below his shoulder was the barrel of the gun. He was cradling the stock with both hands.

The gun had been resting in the corner of the cabin next to his bunk the whole time we'd been back but none of us had paid any attention to it.

Obviously, I didn't want him to have the gun. I mean, he was saying *watch out for the bear* in his sleep just a little while ago.

Do I try to take it from him right now?

He looks like he's asleep.

Or, do I wake him up and ask him for it?

Is the safety on? I don't know.

Is it loaded? I don't know.

He's been confused since he hit his head.

He's got a gun.

He's big and strong.

He has a temper.

Not a good combination.

*You don't walk toward an angry, confused person who has a gun.*

But I couldn't leave Billy to deal with this on his own.

I took a breath.

Mr. Dodge shifted slightly in his bunk, his eyes still closed.

The padding I needed for my kneepads was leaning against the wall next to Billy's bunk.

If I could get it, at least I'd be able to finish preparing the canoe, but what if Mr. Dodge woke up while I was getting the padding? What if he thought I was the bear he'd been calling out about in his sleep?

I stood still—thinking. Thinking. Thinking. Thinking.

Is this a chance worth taking?

No, I thought. It's not. I'll just cut a couple pieces from my own sleeping pad. I'd have to partially unpack the canoe to get to it and that would take time.

Time. How long had I been here?

Billy.

He had to be wondering where I was.

He was holding that canoe in the water.

Probably getting tired.

Get back to Billy, I thought, and we can deal with this crazy gun scene together.

I took a silent step backwards and then another and another until I was out on the porch.

I closed the door gently and turned and ran back down the trail to the river.

I broke through the trees at the edge of the gravel bar.

I sucked in a breath.

Both Billy and the canoe were gone.

# CHAPTER 32

# I TUMBLED over the side of the canoe into the water.

My already-cold body was shocked by the sudden submersion. And even though I'd managed to keep my head above the water, my lungs sucked in a big gasp of air just as a little wave surged over my chin and I inhaled a mouthful of silty water.

I coughed and gasped and kicked my way to the side of the canoe and grabbed it, thankful that I'd left my rubber boots on shore so I wouldn't have to contend with them trying to drag me to the bottom.

I needed to carry out my plan before the canoe got too heavy with water.

No way could I keep my eyes open under water. Even if I could, I wouldn't be able to see anything through all the silt.

I could feel the current tugging my dangling legs, so I knew that if my plan worked the canoe would start drifting and I'd have to somehow deal with that drift. I scooted around to the tip of the bow. The bow rope was stretched out in the water, running alongside the canoe and downstream.

*The time is now. You wait and it will pass. And you'll be right where you are.*

I grabbed the bow rope, sucked in a big breath of air, squeezed my eyes shut, and then pushed downward.

I clutched the rope with one hand and with the other followed the curve of the canoe until it merged with the branch holding it captive. The river was pressing in on my ears and the current was tugging my legs downstream. My feet bumped into the log that the branch was coming from, and I pushed back with the bottoms of both feet, hoping to gain some purchase. My free hand probed the spot where the branch held the canoe. I stuck my fingers through the hole. If there was enough room for a couple of my fingers, then I should be able to wiggle and push and pull the canoe until it was set free.

Now my lungs were screaming for air. I pushed up on the canoe but it didn't move.

No. Come on. Move.

I pushed again.

Nothing.

I needed air, and I needed it now. With my hands I crawled up the rope until my head popped above the surface right at the bow. I sucked in a big breath, grabbed the rim of the canoe and breathed again and again.

The Tanana River had won round one.

But now that I'd been down there, I had an idea.

Shivers ran up my spine.

My feet were blocks of ice.

I crawled back into the boat, and with my numb hands and arms, I started bailing.

Yeah, I was going back in the river, but I needed the boat to be as light as possible.

# AT THE CABIN

## [ONE DAY BEFORE THE FIRE]

"Billy," I yelled.

"Billy."

"Billy."

"Billy."

And then I listened.

But all I heard was the constant flow of the river, which was too soft to drown out a human shout so I listened some more. A raven called out from somewhere but that was all.

Billy.

He had a broken wrist.

He'd been holding the nose of the boat between his legs, just using his good hand to steady it, but if he'd let go, the current would have taken it around the bend. And then bend after bend until it snagged on something or got caught on a sweeper. But he wouldn't have let it go.

But if Billy were in the in the boat, he'd try to land it, like if it started to get away from him and he jumped in, he'd bring it to shore as quickly as he could. But it'd be hard to paddle with only one good arm.

Would he have taken off on purpose? And left me with his dad? It was a possibility. Maybe he thought he would be better at getting help even with only one good arm, since I was really scared of that old canoe sinking and me drowning because of it. I knew a disaster waiting to happen when it was staring me in the face and that old canoe was one of them. Twice he'd threatened to go for help himself if I wasn't willing.

Or, did he lose the boat somehow and was now trying to get it back to shore? Maybe.

"Billy," I yelled again. "Billy. Billy. Billy."

But I heard nothing beyond the river noise, except for my heart, which was pounding in my ears.

If he was bringing it to shore he'd be just downstream.

Unless.

Unless he'd flipped it. Then he'd be in the river without a life vest.

*Look. Look at everything.*

I scanned the bank on the far shore but saw nothing. Downstream was clear until the bend in the river cut off my view.

Upstream? There's no way he could paddle upstream with a broken wrist. But I looked anyway. The river was clear for as far as I could see, which wasn't that far because there was a bend about a quarter mile away.

*Keep looking.*

Then I saw them. First one, and then another. And another. And another. Then a whole line of them. They were faint, but they were there. I'd been so focused on the water that I hadn't looked at everything.

The line of bear tracks came out of the woods about fifty yards upstream, crossed the gravel bar, and ended at the water just above where Billy and the canoe had been.

# CHAPTER 33

**I SLIPPED** over the side of the canoe but this time on the side closest to the shore. I pulled on the rim of the boat as I worked my way toward the stern, tugging it toward shore, trying to get it into the shallowest water possible.

With the tail end of the canoe now in waist high water, I lifted the canoe and rocked it side to side. Then I tried pulling the canoe toward me but it wouldn't budge.

Still stuck.

Stuck.

*Higher. You need to lift it higher.*

"I know," I said. But I was relieved that I was thinking the same thing as my dad's voice.

I lifted the stern again, and then, instead of rocking it, I put my shoulder under it and started walking toward the bow, keeping the canoe raised up as high as I could. But as the water got deeper, even though I was holding the canoe up, its height above the water wasn't getting any greater. I was three quarters of the way toward the bow, but now I was standing on my tippy toes to keep my chin above the water and the river was trying to drag me downstream.

I let the canoe fall off my shoulder and then grabbed the rim.

The Tanana River had won round two.

*Push up from under. All the way under. It's your only hope.*

Under.

Dark water. Freezing cold water.

A submerged tree.

My worst fear was getting pinned between the log and the canoe, but after my last plan failed, I knew I'd need to use the log for leverage if wanted any chance of freeing the canoe.

And then I thought, the paddle.

Use the old paddle as a lever. Wedge it between the log and the canoe and try to pry the canoe free. I reached over the side of the canoe and grabbed the paddle that was lying in the water that had already collected in the bottom of the canoe.

I knew I couldn't lose the paddle, but if I couldn't free the canoe, then the paddle was useless. But if I freed the canoe and lost the paddle, that would be bad, too.

"Okay," I said. "Here goes." I sucked in a breath and then pushed myself under. With my eyes closed, I followed the bottom of the canoe with my free hand until it merged with the branch attached to the log.

Next, I jammed the handle of the paddle in the spot where the branch met the boat before the current took me downstream. Somehow, I had to get some leverage, so I wrapped my upper-body around the blade of the paddle and pushed downward.

At first nothing happened, but I kept pushing and felt a little movement, so I pushed harder. My chest was on fire. I couldn't keep this up much longer without sucking river water into my lungs.

One final push, and then I'd have to go up for air. I leaned heavily downward, felt the upward movement of the paddle, and then there was no tension. I sensed something moving above me, so I pushed upward and surfaced. I lunged for the canoe as the current started taking it and managed to grab the tip of the bow with my free hand. I had to get this boat turned toward shore where all my gear was. I threw the paddle into the canoe, and that's when I saw it. When I was underwater, I'd thought all the pressure release I'd felt came from the canoe getting freed.

But now, staring at what was left of the canoe paddle—just the blade and about one foot of the handle—my heart sank.

I tried turning the boat by facing toward shore and kicking with my legs while holding onto the bow of the canoe, but the current kept carrying me farther downriver.

All I had was a cooking pot.

A piece of a paddle.

My kneepads.

A water bottle.

My soaked clothes.

A survival kit in my fanny pack.

I was stuck in the middle of the river without a life vest, and the river didn't care.

# AT THE CABIN

## [ONE DAY BEFORE THE FIRE]

I ran downriver on the gravel bar until it ended. Then I bushwhacked along the bank. Blueberry bushes tangled my legs in the places where they grew thick.

I hit a stretch of spruce forest where the brush wasn't as thick, but there were trees hanging in the water where the bank had collapsed. Sweepers that Billy would've had to avoid if he'd been in the canoe.

I peered down at the water, thankful that I didn't see the canoe pinned to one of the sweepers.

I kept scanning the far shore, hoping to see Billy and the boat—a spot of white against the green of the forest.

But the opposite shore was all green.

I stopped to yell his name and listened but heard nothing.

And then I thought about the bear tracks.

They ended at the water.

A bear chasing a canoe?

Maybe?

But a bear would come ashore wherever it wanted, so just because I didn't see the canoe didn't mean the bear couldn't be close by.

So, I kept calling for Billy, figuring my voice would also warn the bear if it were still in the area.

I was approaching the first bend now, and the berry bushes, dwarf birch and wild rose formed a solid wall of chest-high vegetation. I beat my way through, swimming with my arms, my rubber boots slip-sliding forward on a mat of bouncy dead brush.

I had to keep the river in view. I was about twenty feet

above the water. At least there were no sweepers on this stretch of the bend. Just brush.

A rose branch full of thorns raked the side of my face making it feel like it was on fire. I rubbed my cheek with my hand and kept going.

I was at the tip of the bend where the river was making a sharp curve, almost doubling back on itself. Around the bend the forest started again. A mix of birch, spruce and aspen. Several spruce were laying on the water extending into the river, their roots keeping them anchored to shore.

A small army of sweepers bouncing in the current, ready to stop, and then sink, anything in their paths.

"Billy!" I yelled. "Billy! Billy! Billy!"

"Over here," Billy called back. His voice was faint but I'd heard it.

I scanned the river but saw nothing. But I couldn't see every part of the river from where I was standing. The sweepers—I counted four of them on the first part of the bend—blocked some of my view.

At least if Billy were yelling that meant he was breathing.

"Keep yelling," I shouted. "I can't see you!"

"Over here," Billy called out again. "Quick. Before it's too late."

# CHAPTER 34

**THE RIVER** not only wasn't stopping but somehow the current was carrying me across to the opposite bank while it propelled me downstream. I kept kicking, trying to turn the boat toward the shore where all my gear was, but the current was more than cancelling out my kicks. Without a life vest to keep me afloat, my arms were turning to rubber from not only gripping the boat but from pulling myself up enough to keep my head from going under. The silty water was dragging me down.

The boat swung around so the bow now faced downstream. I scooted along the side of the canoe because I didn't like the feeling of my back facing downriver. If the canoe ran into another log, I could be trapped between it and the canoe. My arms started to give out and my head slipped under water, and I came up choking.

I coughed and hacked silty water out of my throat.

*Get in the boat. Now. Over the stern.*

My head slipped under again and I pulled myself up so my chin was just above the water.

*Focus. Don't let the river win.*

Hand over hand, I worked myself along the rim of the canoe and my head slipped under two more times before I finally reached the stern. Then I shifted one hand to the opposite rim.

I knew I needed to go right over the center, or else I could end up flipping the canoe.

I pushed down on both rims and rose up to my waist and then fell forward into the canoe and smashed my head against one of the struts. The bottom of the canoe was awash with ankle-deep water. I grabbed what was left of my paddle and gripped the one-foot-long handle with both hands and paddled on the right side of the canoe, which turned me left toward the closest point of land. It was on the opposite side of the river from my gear, but I needed to get to shore so I could try to plug the leak.

I glanced over my shoulder from where I'd come and already the birch grove where my gear was piled up was turning into a tiny speck. The river was at least a quarter mile wide, plus I'd been carried downstream by the swift current. If only that bow rope had been long enough to tie off to a tree before I'd freed the canoe.

My teeth chattered. Shivers rocked my spine.

Freeze to death, I thought.

I could freeze to death in the middle of a forest fire.

Even though my arms were mush, I kept paddling. But it was hard to paddle with such a short handle. I had to reach way over the side of the boat even from the very back of the canoe where it was narrowest. My knees ached from pressing against the knobby wood of the bottom frame. I could see my kneepads toward the front of the boat but didn't want to take the time to move forward to get them.

My weight back here, being the only weight in the boat, besides all the water, made the bow ride up higher, which made the water pool in the stern of the canoe. I dropped my paddle and bailed furiously until the water in the canoe came down to a few inches.

I picked up the tiny paddle and got to work getting the canoe closer to shore.

Birches. I need more birches to land in.

With the constant movement of bailing and paddling I was still cold, but not as cold as when I had first dove into the canoe after being in the river.

Movement.

As long as I was cold and wet, I had to keep moving. My arms were burning with pain but at least they were still working.

Flames, set back from the river, visible through the charred spruce trees, filled the horizon.

I could land anywhere there aren't flames, I thought. But then I remembered the massive burnt tree that had fallen on the canoe.

Birches would be better. Once I made it to shore, I wanted to be there for as little time as possible.

My plan after I got to shore.

Flip the canoe to let the water drain out.

Somehow fix the hole.

Keep on going.

Without my gear.

Without my boots.

Without much of a paddle.

Without much of anything.

# AT THE CABIN

## [ONE DAY BEFORE THE FIRE]

Billy straddled the front of the canoe—one foot in the river, the other on the narrow strip of rocky shore before the bank turned steep—holding it from crashing into the sweeper.

The back end of the canoe started to swing into the current, and Billy laid himself against the outside of the canoe and edged it back toward shore.

"I'll grab the back of the canoe," I yelled. "Just hang on." The bank was steep, and I didn't want to fall into the river just above a sweeper where the current could trap me against it.

I'd have to use the brush to climb down. I'd learned once not to use brush to climb down steep slopes. Out on Bear Island I'd fallen forty feet because I'd grabbed at some berry bushes to climb down a steep slope and they'd given way.

*Sometimes you have to do one unsafe thing to keep something worse from happening.*

I faced away from the river, got onto my knees and edged my legs over the bank, turning my head to keep the small branches from poking me in the eyes.

I hugged the bank. I hugged it hard.

A branch from a wild rose plant found me just under the chin but I just kept sliding and gripping and pressing, trying to slow myself so when my feet hit the rocky shore I wouldn't crumble and break a leg. I was speeding up now.

My cheek screamed from the rose thorns.

Somewhere during the fall I'd closed my eyes to protect them.

My feet hit. I fell, rolled sideways, and felt a thud on the side of my head as it smashed into the rocky shore.

I opened my eyes, turned toward the canoe, and grabbed it as I stood up because it was right there—I'd almost landed in it.

"I got it," I yelled. "Get out of the water."

Billy leaped to shore as the current kept up its fight to take the canoe from us. I shifted my hands from holding the back of the canoe to the center, and I snugged it into shore—something you needed two good arms to do.

"I saw the bear tracks."

"Yeah." Billy was holding his broken wrist against his chest. "I got out of there just in time. I was facing downriver and didn't see the bear until it was almost on top of me."

Then Billy told me about the bear abandoning the chase halfway across the river and swimming to the opposite shore, but by that time the current had taken Billy around the first bend, and with his broken wrist, every stroke had been excruciating.

He'd been trying to avoid the row of four sweepers, but he'd underestimated the power of the current.

My arms were turning to rubber from holding the canoe in the current. I didn't want to drag the boat ashore on the rocks because that might damage the bottom. "We need to unload the boat so I can get it out of the water." I glanced over my shoulder at the steep bank I'd slid down. "Then we'll have to figure out how to get it around this sweeper."

# CHAPTER 35

**I HAD** the canoe out of the water on the shore opposite from where my gear was and way downriver. The oval-shaped hole, about four inches long and an inch or two wide, ran between two of the bottom supports on the floor of the canoe.

I might've made it bigger getting the canoe unstuck, but if I hadn't freed the canoe, it'd still be caught, maybe filled with so much water that no way would it budge.

Tradeoffs.

Unexpected tradeoffs.

Like if I had known that to save the canoe, I'd end up losing all my gear, my boots, and most of the handle of my only paddle, I'm not sure what I would've done. I mean, given the forest fires raging, the river was really the safest place to be. But could someone walk the riverbank and just get in the water and swim if they got to places that were just too hot and dangerous to walk through?

But swimming would make you super cold, unless you had a wetsuit or a dry suit, neither of which I had. Plus, I knew I wouldn't survive long in the river without a life vest. The weight of the silt on my clothes would drag me down.

I wished I could get my gear, but that would have taken lining the canoe against the current and then trying to cross the river with a tiny paddle. And that would have taken time. Time that I didn't have. Sure, if I were on a trip that didn't involve trying to save two people's lives, then yeah, I'd probably try to get the gear.

But if I took the time to try to get the gear and one of them didn't make it, I couldn't live with that. But not getting the gear was risky, too.

All I had in my puny emergency kit that was stuffed inside a Ziploc bag inside a small fanny pack was:

Pocket knife

Lighter

Matches

Two Clif Bars

Fishing line

Two fishing hooks

Besides my clothes, I also had one water bottle, kneepads, and a cooking/bailing pot.

Under normal circumstances when a person is stranded, being able to start a fire is essential. But I was in the middle of a forest fire. I'd packed this kit like I was still stranded on Bear Island. A roll of duct tape would have been good for temporary repairs, but I didn't have one. I didn't have anything useful except the Clif Bars, and maybe the knife.

Except.

Wait.

Yeah, I knew what was in the kit.

But what about what the kit was packed in?

I eyed the small red nylon fanny pack and the Ziploc bag.

A shiver ran through my body, reminding me that I was wet and freezing cold despite being in the middle of a forest fire.

Maybe I *would* need a fire to dry out and warm up before getting back in the canoe.

I shivered again.

At the edge of the birch forest I stripped bark from a tree. Then I picked up some bone-dry sticks. I stripped more bark and collected more sticks.

Just a quick fire to partially dry off.

Fix the canoe.

Dry off.

Go.

A few feet from the edge of the river, I crumpled the birch bark and then piled small sticks on top of it. With the lighter I lit the birch bark, and it started crackling and then bellowing some black smoke as the flames climbed upward, catching the sticks on fire. I jogged to the edge of the forest and collected more sticks. Back at the fire, I piled them on.

The warmth was instant on my face and hands. I stripped off my long-sleeved T-shirt, wrung it out and set it on the sandy gravel next to the fire. Then I did the same with my pants, underwear, and socks.

Yeah, I was naked, but the fire was drying me off and I was starting to feel warm, which made me sleepy.

I drank what was left in my water bottle, then filled the pot with river water so the silt would settle, and I'd have more drinking water.

I alternated holding my shirt, pants, and underwear close to the flames, trying to get the maximum benefit from the fire. There was still smoke in the air from the forest fires, but I'd been so focused on getting the canoe unstuck and then getting it to shore, I hadn't really noticed it—like it had become normal for me to live in a yellow haze where ash rained down and charred trees fell in the wind. But now that I had noticed, I also noticed that my throat and nose, were both feeling raw.

Without my bandana to act as a filter, I'd been sucking smoke for a while now.

I piled more sticks on the fire and then faced the overturned canoe.

"I will fix you," I said.

I glanced at the nub of paddle I had left and shook my head. "I wish I could fix you."

I grabbed the nylon fanny pack.

It had straps.

And a buckle.

I walked back to the fire and grabbed my shirt. It was still damp, but it wasn't soaked.

I put it on and then grabbed my underwear. They were still soaked, so I stuck a stick upright in the ground close to the fire, hung my underwear on it and turned back to the canoe.

Maybe by the time I finished trying out my repair idea, they'd be dry enough to wear.

# AT THE CABIN

## [ONE DAY BEFORE THE FIRE]

We'd unloaded the canoe and piled the dry bags against the bank. I'd carefully lifted it out of the water and set it down on the narrow strip of rocky shore between the steep bank and the river.

We'd unloaded the canoe and piled the dry bags against the bank. I'd carefully lifted it out of the water and set it down on the narrow strip of rocky shore between the steep bank and the river.

I glanced at the vertical bank. "Try to get the canoe up there?" I shook my head. "No way." I rubbed the rose thorn scratches on my cheek. I could feel the raised lines—a bunch of them running from just below my eye to my jawbone. My head throbbed where it had connected with the rocky shore.

Billy pointed upstream. "If we can get the canoe and all the gear far enough away from the sweeper, you could just paddle around it."

I looked upstream. A jumble of rocks and cut bank took up the shore all the way to the next sweeper about a hundred yards away. "I could carry it to that next sweeper and launch from there."

"I can help carry the dry bags," Billy said. "And you might be able to float the canoe for part of it." Billy pointed to the rope attached to the bow. "You know. Pull it along against the current where there aren't any sharp rocks or logs poking out."

I gave the rope a tug. It was tied tightly. I stretched it out. "Plenty of length to play with." I stared upriver again. About halfway between the two sweepers were some jagged rocks. "I'll float it till I get to those rocks. Pull it out. And then float it again if it looks good."

I picked up the canoe, braced it against my thighs, and took a couple of slow steps toward the river.

I set the canoe in the water, keeping one hand on the side of the canoe while I grabbed the bow rope with my other hand. Then I turned to Billy. "Okay, here goes."

I choked up on the rope so only about five feet separated me from the canoe, and then let go of the side of the canoe. The back end of the canoe immediately flared out into the current so the canoe sat at about a forty-five-degree angle to the shore.

When I pulled, it created more resistance, and the current hit the boat broadside. The more I pulled, the more the boat flared out.

*You've got to bring the stern of the canoe in line with the bow.*

I followed the rope down to the canoe, grabbed the side of the canoe and pulled it toward me until the canoe was lined up along the bank.

Less resistance, I thought. There's way less resistance when the canoe isn't broadside to the current but how to keep it like that on the rope was the question.

I moved back toward the bow of the boat, and the stern—the back end—swung out again. I moved to the stern, and the bow swung out. But when I held the boat from the middle with both hands, it stayed where I wanted it to stay.

Billy must've been watching me the whole time because just as I was starting to understand what I needed to do, I felt a nudge on my shoulder, and when I turned to face him, he had just what I needed—a loose piece of rope.

# CHAPTER 36

**WITH THE** canoe turned upright, I fitted the fanny pack that I'd stuffed with sand on top of the hole, wedging it between two of the five pieces of wood that made up the bottom frame. Then I worked the fanny pack straps under the pieces of wood and cinched them together over the fanny pack, making it look like the bottom frame of the canoe was wearing the fanny pack, which it now was.

I knew it wasn't a complete seal. I thought about poking some holes in the bottom and running rope or fishing line through them to make things tighter, but I didn't want to put any more holes in the canoe.

I'd just have to keep an eye on the fanny pack.

And, I thought, I'll sit in the back of the canoe so my weight will be farther away from the bow and it will ride higher in the water.

I wouldn't be able to control the canoe as well as I had when I'd knelt in the middle, and with no weight in the bow I could get blown around. And, the patch in the back might leak from my weight, making the canoe ride lower in the stern.

I remembered how much more stable the canoe was with the ballast rocks. It seemed like days or weeks since I'd had those ballast rocks but really, it'd only been hours. With all this smoke and not being able to see the sun at all, I'd lost track of time.

Was it midnight?

Or two in the morning?

Or was it already noon the next day?

And in my new reality so far, sleep just didn't exist.

Three days going on four. That was my guess about how long I'd been paddling. I'd only slept a few hours on the first night and had been up straight since then.

When I stayed with the Dodges, I'd had some sleepless nights and once found Mrs. Dodge in the kitchen way past midnight.

"Mrs. Dodge, I hope you don't mind. I couldn't sleep and I was hungry, and I thought eating something might help me fall asleep."

She smiled at me and said, "Not at all, Tom. You know you can help yourself to anything. There's leftover pie on the counter."

"Thanks," I said. "You couldn't sleep either?"

"I've got a lot on my mind," she said, "but I think I've figured it all out." She stared into here coffee cup. "Not that it helps all that much."

"Ever since my Uncle Jim has been in touch," I said, "I've been thinking a lot about Michigan. I don't want to go." I felt my eyes getting hot and rubbed them before the tears could escape. "I'd do almost anything to stay in Alaska."

Mrs. Dodge looked me in the eye. "Change is hard. It's scary. Sometimes it doesn't even matter if it is a change you want or don't want, it's still scary."

Now it was just me and the river and the burning trees on either side with the occasional stands of birch forest that had somehow escaped the full force of the fire.

I put the rest of my emergency kit items back into the Ziploc bag, except for one of the Clif Bars, which I'd eaten.

My throat was raw from the smoke, so I poured some water into my water bottle and drank it, and then refilled it with what was left in the pot.

My underwear was still pretty wet, but my pants had dried some so I put them back on.

Underwear.

Kneepads.

Cooking pot.

Water bottle.

Broken paddle.

Ziploc with emergency kit items.

The kneepads were easy enough to know what to do with.

But where to put the rest of the stuff?

I took the other Clif Bar and stuffed it into my back pocket.

The pot and water bottle I decided to keep loose in the boat.

I sealed the Ziploc Bag and worked the end under one of the ribs of the canoe and pulled it until a third of the bag was on one side of the rib, and the rest of it with the lighter, matches, fishing lures and line was on the other side.

I coughed again and then spit black saliva onto the sand. I wished I had my wet bandana to filter the nasty, smoky air.

Black Saliva Beach. That's what I'll call this spot. I didn't even want to think about what my lungs might look like now.

My fire had burned down to coals. I dumped a few pots of river water on it. I didn't want to start a forest fire within the forest fire, if that was even possible.

I brushed the sand and silt off my feet and pulled my damp socks on, and yeah, I wished I had my boots.

Gently, I lifted the bow of the canoe and set it in the river.

I grabbed the nub-of-a-paddle I had left and put it in the boat.

I coughed and spit more black saliva. I gave the beach one last glance and noticed that I'd left my wet underwear hanging on a stick by what used to be my fire, like an I surrender flag.

"I don't need those," I said. I spit more black saliva and then I lifted the stern of the canoe and was about to set it in the river and shove off when I paused.

I set the stern back on the beach and turned toward the underwear.

# AT THE CABIN
## (ONE DAY BEFORE THE FIRE)

I didn't know how long a piece of rope I'd need on the stern of the canoe. I didn't want to limit myself by cutting a piece that was too small, so I coiled up a bunch of the fifty-foot long rope, set it in the canoe, and tied it off, leaving about thirty feet free to use.

"Once you tie your stuff in the canoe," Billy said, "you could cut the rope and the rest of it you'll have for your stern rope." He pointed to the back of the canoe. "That way, if you need to do this again on the trip, you'll be ready."

"Yeah, that sounds like a good idea. But first, let's see if it even works."

I gripped both ropes and let the side of the canoe go. The stern immediately flared out, so I pulled in the slack on the stern rope until the back end lined up with the front end, and then I just held the ropes, getting a feel for how the boat would react.

Two streams of water, forming an inverted V ran away from the canoe on both sides of the bow. I took a couple of steps forward and the canoe moved with me.

I looked over my shoulder at Billy. "This is way better."

"Good deal," he said. "I'll start moving the gear."

I walked a few more steps and the back of the canoe flared in toward the shore, so I let out a little slack and it lined back up with the bow.

*Lining. You are lining a boat. Adjust. Adjust. Adjust. And anticipate. A river changes and you have to change, too.*

When I reached the rocks, I took in the slack on the ropes until the canoe was next to the shore. I hoisted it up, rested it on my thighs, and carried it around the rocks, and then put it back in the water and lined it the rest of the way to just below the next sweeper.

I set the canoe down gently, jogged back to the pile of gear and made a couple of trips with Billy until we had all the gear next to the canoe, and then repacked it.

"I can't climb the bank here," Billy said. "Not with my broken wrist."

I glanced up and down the river. There wasn't an easy way to get above the bank that I could see without having to swim around a bend. "Ride with me," I said. "After I paddle around that sweeper, I'll pull into shore at the first spot where the bank isn't so steep and you can't just walk right up it."

Billy looked at the canoe and then at me. "The thing I was looking most forward to was you and me paddling this canoe. Remember?"

I nodded. The last thing I wanted to do was take off downriver alone.

Billy went on. "We should do this. My dad's been alone for a long time now."

"Your dad told me he wanted to make things right with you on this trip." I paused. "He told me I've got to get help so he can make it right not only out here, but back home."

Billy reached into his pocket and pulled out a crumpled piece of paper.

"What's that?" I asked.

"It's from my mom. I found it on my dad's bunk just before we headed out to pack the canoe." Billy handed it to me. "He doesn't know I have it." Billy shook his head. "Just when I thought things were looking up at home."

# CHAPTER 37

**I DUNKED** the underwear in the river and then rung them out.

And no, I wouldn't have believed it if someone had told me a couple weeks ago that someday soon I'd be willingly wearing my own underwear over my face.

But hey, you do what you need to do to survive. At least they were my underwear and not someone else's.

And, I'd rinsed them in the river.

Since I liked breathing more than I liked choking on smoke, I figured it was a pretty good trade off even if I had been wearing them ever since I left the cabin.

Through the waist opening, I pulled the underwear over my head and then let one of the leg openings rest on my nose. The wet cloth hung limp around my face. I tucked the elastic of the leg opening around my ears to keep the whole contraption from falling around my neck.

The relief was immediate. My throat was still raw and scratchy—like someone had taken a piece of sandpaper to it—from all the smoke I'd sucked in since I'd been without my bandana, but now the air I was inhaling was cooler, and not as smoky tasting.

I lifted the stern of the canoe and set it into the river. In shin-high water, I gave the boat a push and jumped in.

My feet were immediately cold from my wet socks clinging to them. I knelt on my kneepads. Without the yellow dry bag to straddle, I had to kneel straight up, sit on my heels or do something in between.

I grabbed the tiny paddle and realized I'd have to kneel straight up so I could lean far enough over the side to actually get the paddle blade into the river. But I couldn't lean too much or else the whole canoe would lean. I had to reach with my arms as far as I could, then lean with my body the rest of the way. Even though it was more taxing on me to have to rely mostly on my arms, when I leaned farther with my body the canoe felt less stable, and I didn't want to go into the river again. Ever.

I did a quick scan of the interior of the canoe.

The bow rope was coiled up, snug in the front of the canoe. On the left rim, just back from the bow, the splint was holding the broken rim together. Then came the red-fanny-pack patch, which so far, after less than a minute on the river, seemed to be holding.

Wedged underneath one of the ribs, within reaching distance, was the plastic bag with the rest of the survival kit. Just in front of my knees, the pot and my full water bottle sat loose. To my right, the blue patch from my rain pants was keeping the river out. And behind me, I could feel the stern rope pressed against my toes.

Try to keep close to shore, I thought, as I paddled. Not so close that I had to deal with dodging sweepers, but if the canoe started to take on water, I didn't want to be way out in the middle.

A steady cold settled into my feet, but thankfully the rest of my body just felt chilled. The work of paddling was keeping me from freezing. And the underwear-smoke-mask was allowing me to breathe without continually coughing.

The shore was a mix of smoldering spruce snags devoid of branches and needles, and birch that had been partially charred and occasionally completely burned. There was nothing left of the understory in most places. I didn't see any flames, but I was pretty sure the ground reaching back from the river was hot. The shore on the far side of the river appeared to be equally fried.

Up ahead, I could see the landscape changing. The flats that stretched away from the river on both sides were being replaced with bluffs.

Mostly blackened bluffs.

Paddle.

Paddle.

Paddle.

Switch sides.

Paddle.

Paddle.

Paddle.

That was my pattern as long as there were no obstacles.

Then I noticed some water in the canoe around the edge of the gray flooring. The fanny pack was mostly plugging up the hole but there must've been some space where the water was coming through. Then it was spreading out under the gray flooring. And now that enough water had collected, it was flowing out at the edges.

*You can always bail.*

I'd have to keep an eye on the water level. One more thing to watch in addition to all the hazards in the river.

The base of the first bluff was approaching. Maybe a quarter mile and I'd be there.

I can do this, I told myself.

Yeah, I was hungry.

Yeah, I was cold.

Yeah, I'd lost all my gear.

Yeah, I didn't know much about paddling a canoe. Especially one full of holes.

Yeah, I hadn't slept for at least three or four days. I was losing count.

Yeah, I wanted to stop and sleep.

But I kept paddling like a zombie would. Like the walking dead who lived on in their *walking dead* forms, I was the *paddling dead*.

Islands stretched out from the bluff. Charred stands of trees poked up from the silty river.

*Pick a channel now. Aim for it. The current won't stop.*

My heart beat a hole through my damp shirt. The river bottom must be bumpy here to have so many islands.

Stick by the base of the bluff, I thought. Aim for the center of the channel between the bluff and the first charred island.

I paddled hard on the right side of the canoe repeatedly, which moved me to the left.

Approaching the channel, I hoped I'd made the right choice.

# AT THE CABIN

## [ONE DAY BEFORE THE FIRE]

I read the letter Billy handed me.

> *Dear Ted,*
> *I hope you and Billy are having some good times together and I hope the news of our pending divorce doesn't stress him out too much when you break it to him. I want this to have the least impact on Billy as possible. Spend your time out there with him rebuilding your relationship so you're on a solid foundation when you return. I know it'll be a big adjustment when Billy moves to Seattle with me but with your work schedule, I just don't see any other way to do this. I'm glad you were able to get the time off work to do this trip.*
> *Love,*
> *Debbie*

I handed the letter back to Billy. "Even though you might have to move, your dad still cares about you."

Billy kicked a rock into the river. "I just need to take care of him until you get us some help."

"We better go. You get in first," I said. I held the stern of the canoe steady.

Billy worked his way to the bow and settled in on top of the bag with the tent and tarp.

The only thing holding back the canoe now was me. I sucked in some air. "Okay. Here goes." I pushed off with my legs, hopped in and knelt.

I dipped the old wooden paddle into the water and pulled. The canoe wanted to point directly downstream and ride with the current, but I needed to get at least halfway across to avoid the sweeper that Billy had almost gotten pinned against.

"Flare your paddle out at the end of a stroke," Billy said, "and it'll help with steering."

I dipped my paddle in the downstream side and flared it out and the nose of the canoe shifted and pointed across the river. Then I paddled, but I kept having to steer to correct the course. We were getting closer and closer to the sweeper, and we still weren't clear of it, and the current wasn't going to let up, so I doubled down.

Paddle. Paddle. Paddle.

Steer.

Paddle. Paddle. Paddle.

Steer.

I kept up the pattern, and slowly we made our way to the middle of the river and passed the sweeper.

"I'm going to aim for that sandy spot where the bank isn't so steep." I said, "Let me know if you see any rocks or logs, or anything sharp."

"You got it," Billy said. "All clear so far."

My knees ached from being pressed against the knobby wood, and we'd only been on the river for maybe twenty minutes.

The bow of the canoe nosed the shore gently, and Billy hopped out and held the boat. I gripped both sides of the canoe, stood up, and stepped into shin-high water and then onto shore. I rubbed my knees. "I need to make those knee pads before I go any further."

"I'll hold the boat while you make them, but then you need to go, and I've got to get back to my dad," Billy said.

"Your dad," I said. "In all this craziness, I almost forgot. I need to go back with you. He was asleep but was holding the gun across his chest. Hugging it."

# CHAPTER 38

## (BILLY AND HIS DAD)

"**DAD,**" I said. "We've got to go now."

"Save yourself, Billy," my dad countered. "You'll be better off without me. Now get out of here, before this place goes up in flames."

"Is this the image you want to leave me with?" I slammed the orange plastic sled onto the floor. "Refusing to help me save you?"

"I don't want to you to die trying to save me. You go, now!"

"Yesterday, you said you wanted to do better," I argued. "Now you're back to being the same old you, trying to control everything with your anger. You want to do something different, then let me call the shots here. And if you die and I don't, at least I'll go forward knowing that I did everything in my power to save you instead of my last few moments with you being like most of the times we've had together. I—"

"Billy, I—"

"I'm not finished. You said you wanted to change, and if that's true you've got to start now because we may both be dead in a couple of hours."

My dad took in a big breath and exhaled. He looked down at his leg and shook his head. Then said softly, "I'll do what you say. Just promise me that if it comes down to dying with me or saving yourself that you'll save yourself."

"Fair enough," I agreed. "Now, we need to move."

# CHAPTER 39

I THREADED my way between the two-hundred-foot-high bluff and the closest island, which was flat and burned. The bluff was steep. A patchwork of charred vegetation and greenery covered the almost vertical face.

The river was bending around to the left, and the bluff was giving way to some burned up hills. Even here, the birch trees were blackened snags. I didn't know why I'd seen birches spared upriver as compared to right here but was thankful that they hadn't been burning, so I'd had a place to fix my boat.

My arms were spaghetti from paddling with the tiny paddle. A steady ache settled into my shoulders from the constant reaching. There was about an inch of water on top of the gray flooring, but I just kept paddling.

I rounded the bend and could feel the headwind tugging at the underwear covering my face. But worse, it was trying to blow the bow of the boat sideways. I kept digging in on the right side trying to push the bow to the left, but the wind was relentless. There was a river of wind flowing on top of the water in the opposite direction that I needed to go.

But the wind was doing more than that. It was starting to kick up some waves, which were washing against the canoe.

I tried to keep the canoe from going broadside to the waves.

Paddle.

Paddle.

Paddle.

The wind on my damp clothes was cancelling out any warmth I was generating from paddling. Shivers ran up my spine. My fingers grew numb and my feet turned into blocks of ice. But I kept paddling. I couldn't see any flames, but the smoke was still pretty thick. Except that way downriver, through the smoke, I thought I spied a patch of blue sky.

Get to the blue, I thought. Get to the blue.

Water was bubbling around the red fanny pack. The waves must be pushing on it, I thought. At some point I'll have to bail.

I kept on paddling.

How much water could this old canoe hold before it sank?

Or how much water could it hold before it'd be impossible to get it to move by paddling?

Another set of charred islands loomed in front of me. At least I was still moving downriver even if the wind had slowed my progress and my boat had taken on some water.

The entrance to the far-left channel looked inviting. The water over there was flat. No waves. I kept digging my scrawny paddle into the river on the right side, shooting for that quiet channel.

I nosed the canoe into the channel and felt immediate relief as the wind died. The charred island to my right was hilly just like the riverbank to the left. It was great not having the wind in my face, but there wasn't much current in this channel either.

*Slough. You are in a slough. Slow moving. Meandering.*

I alternated paddling three times on the left and then three on the right, keeping to the center of the narrow channel.

Slough, I pondered. And now, I remembered what Mr. Dodge had said. Some sloughs were short, but some could wander for miles before rejoining the main river.

Then I remembered that time in third grade when Billy convinced his mom to let us wade into Noyes Slough, which flows behind his house in Fairbanks, to pull out a bicycle Billy had spotted resting on the bottom. We were in freezing water up to our waists, and even though the bike turned out to be a piece of junk, we felt like we'd discovered buried treasure after we'd hauled it onto shore. You couldn't even tell that the water had a current in Noyes Slough.

If I'd had a normal canoe without holes, and normal wind conditions, then being in a slough could really slow me down. But with a headwind, plus the potential for the waves created by the headwind to force more and more water into the big hole in the bottom of the canoe, maybe this slough would get me to where I was going faster than the main river if I paddled—and paddled hard.

I picked up the pace which also helped me warm up. I was starving, so I worked the Clif Bar out of my back pocket, lifted the underwear off my face, and stuffed it in my mouth. Ten minutes later I was hungry again, but since there was nothing I could do about it, I just kept paddling.

Steady. Keep it steady.

For Billy.

That first year after my mom died, I came to school on a lot of days without much of a lunch. My dad was so depressed that he had a hard time even getting to the store. Without me even asking, Billy started sharing his lunches with me. He must've told his parents what was up because it seemed like he always had plenty of food for two people. I still felt bad about arguing with Billy about taking this canoe down the river after all he'd done for me but look at the canoe now. It was falling apart around me, and I didn't have a life vest.

I kept on paddling. The slough wound through the burnt landscape. Some patches of forest were less burnt than others, but mostly, the place was a mess. Big winds would topple a ton of these trees.

The slough was making a sharp bend which I hoped would lead straight back to the river. I flared the blade of my paddle to keep the canoe in the center of the narrow channel. The water now had a greenish tinge to it, unlike the usual gray-brown color of the main river.

I was deep in the bend now. I dug my paddle in trying to pick up the pace, hoping by the time I re-entered the main river, the wind wouldn't be as strong.

I paddled hard again.

"No!" I yelled.

A wall of brown fur emerged from the water in front of me, its mouth dripping with green algae. Then off to the side a smaller moose appeared, like it'd come up from the bottom as well. The big moose now stood knee-deep in the water on the right side of the channel. Just beyond her, the smaller moose stood, its underside touching the water.

I started backpaddling, but I could tell I was already too close. The bigger moose was already stepping toward me with her ears flat against her head.

# AT THE CABIN

## (ONE DAY BEFORE THE FIRE)

"He's still got the gun," Billy whispered, peering into the window next to the door of the cabin.

"Let's go in quietly," I whispered back. "We don't want to startle him."

Billy nodded. "But once we're in there, we'll need to wake him up and then get the gun away from him."

I glanced in through the window. "Do you remember how he was saying watch out for the bear while he was sleeping?"

"Yeah," Billy said.

"Neither of us wants to be mistaken for a bear."

"That's exactly why we have to wake him up." Billy shook his head. "He's got a head injury and he's confused. We can't give him a chance to react to whatever he thinks is around. He might just start firing that thing before he realizes it's just us."

"We need to be close to him," I said. "Like maybe on either side of him. That way when we wake him up, we're not just vague targets across the cabin."

Billy added, "We'll have to be so close to him that he couldn't shoot us if he tried."

The sun was beating down on the little porch. I thought I caught a whiff of smoke, but there was no way Mr. Dodge had built a fire in the woodstove. "Smoke?" I turned to Billy. "You smell that?"

Billy sniffed the air. Then he went down the steps and looked toward the roof. "Maybe?" Billy said. "But there's nothing coming out of the stove pipe that I can see." He shrugged. "No way did he build a fire." And then he walked back up the steps.

I caught another whiff of smoke. Maybe the stove was putting out some odors. That used to happen with our woodstove at home. If creosote had built up inside it, you could smell this smoke-like odor even when there wasn't a fire. My dad used to sweep the chimney two or three times a year, but after my mom died, he let it go and for a long time we just lived with that nasty odor.

It's not my home anymore, I thought. An image of my uncle and the real estate agent he'd hired, who had sold the house, flashed into my mind and my stomach clenched like someone had thrown a punch at me. I didn't want to move to Michigan with Uncle Jim. I just wanted to live in Fairbanks. And Heather was supposed to be moving back to town at the end of the summer. I hadn't seen her since she moved away just after my mom died, but I'd seen pictures of her. We used to play together because our moms were best friends. Now I didn't know if I'd ever see her again.

Billy touched my arm and jolted me out of my thoughts. "Tom," he whispered. "We need to do this. Are you ready?"

I glanced into the window. Mr. Dodge still appeared to be conked out. I nodded. I picked up the two dry bags with food in them that I'd carried back from the canoe. "Yeah. I'm ready."

Billy gently pushed the door open.

# CHAPTER 40

**THE DEEP** water in the center of the slough saved me. The mother moose couldn't rise up and pummel me with her front hooves in water she couldn't stand in. Images of the moose Billy and I had witnessed, protecting her calf from the wolves, up the Olsen, flashed in my brain.

I kept back-paddling even though the moose had stopped advancing. She stood sideways to me on the same side of the channel as her yearling calf.

But now I had another problem.

I couldn't wait all day for the moose to move out of the way. I maneuvered the canoe to the opposite side of the slough and let the stern ground out in shallow water.

Options and choices.

You make a choice from your options.

Sometimes when you need to make a quick choice, you aren't even aware you have options. Like when the moose appeared, I started back-paddling. That was a choice, but I didn't review all the options I had, I just reacted by doing what I thought would save me.

But now, even though I needed to get downriver as quickly as I could, I needed to review my options because making the right choice equaled making the most forward progress. It also equaled, hopefully, not being stomped to death by a moose.

In my mind I listed three:

Wait the moose out.

Line or paddle the boat against the current up the slough back to the river and pick another channel.

Abandon the canoe and walk.

I didn't want to wait. I was already cold and wet, and sitting and waiting would just make me colder. With nothing but socks on my feet, the idea of walking was just plain crazy unless another disaster struck and my already beat-up canoe was totally destroyed.

Then a fourth option popped into my head. I looked over at the moose. The younger one had its head under water, feeding on the plants it could reach. The mother was still standing sideways to me, but her ears weren't flat on her head anymore.

"Moose, I just want to pass by," I explained. "I'll stay on this side of the slough. I promise."

I knew the water was deep right in the middle of the slough. I didn't know for a fact that it was deep everywhere in the middle for the entire length of the slough, but the deep water had stopped the moose when I'd surprised her.

Use the deep water as a barrier, I thought. The safe thing to do would be to turnaround and go back up the slough, or to wait, but when I thought of Billy and what he was up against, I just couldn't take the time to wait or backtrack.

Chances.

Sometimes you have to take a chance.

Sometimes you have to choose the thing that isn't safe.

Not because you are looking for a thrill. Not because you are intentionally doing something stupid. But because someone is counting on you to save their life. Someone you care about more than anyone else you know.

I stepped out of the canoe. My sock-covered feet squished into the mud. The mother moose turned toward me.

"Easy," I whispered to the moose. "Easy now."

I reached into the boat and grabbed the stern rope, then walked forward and grabbed the bowline.

Keep the boat close to shore, I thought. Keep it between me and the moose.

One hundred mud-sucking yards to walk as I lined the canoe.

A shiver grabbed my body and shook me from the neck down.

My heart was beating overtime.

I hoped the moose would stay on her side of the slough. I hoped she somehow knew that I wasn't hunting her calf.

I choked up on both ropes so the canoe didn't have a choice except to stay right next to me as I walked.

The bottoms of my feet sunk into the mud and made these sucking sounds each time I pulled them up to take another step.

After five steps the moose hadn't moved, so I kept going.

I took another step, and her ears flared back.

"Okay," I said softly. "I know you are angry, but I am going to keep going. I need to keep going."

I took another step.

# AT THE CABIN

## (ONE DAY BEFORE THE FIRE)

I set the dry bags by the bench on the wall next to the door and walked to the left side of Mr. Dodge's bunk. Billy was already in position on the right side of the bunk.

Mr. Dodge hadn't woken up, and now here we were.

Part of me wanted to just take the gun from him and be done with it.

Grab it now while he was still asleep.

We could probably have it away from him before he realized what was happening. But when I looked closer, I saw that he had a firm grip and that his finger was pretty close to the trigger.

I looked at Billy and raised my eyebrows, but he was studying his dad's face and didn't respond to my silent *what-do-we-do-now*, gesture.

I waved my hand and that broke Billy's gaze. "What do we do now?" I mouthed.

"Dad," Billy said, while putting a hand on his shoulder. "Dad."

Mr. Dodge shifted his body a little bit. His forehead and cheeks looked all sweaty.

"Mr. Dodge," I said, while touching his other shoulder. His shirt was damp, too.

"We're gonna take the gun, Dad," Billy said softly. "You don't need it right now." But then Billy didn't try to take the gun. He just stood there.

"Mr. Dodge," I said. "It's time to wake up." I gave his shoulder another nudge, and then shook it.

"The bear. The bear," Mr. Dodge mumbled. Then his eyes

popped open, and at the same time his hands closed more tightly around the gun.

"Dad," Billy said. "It's okay. It's only me and Tom. There's no bear."

Mr. Dodge looked at Billy. Then he turned and looked at me.

"Will you please let go of the gun?" I asked, pointing my hand at the barrel.

Mr. Dodge glanced down and raised his eyebrows. "How'd I get this?"

"After we carried the gear to the shore to load the canoe, Tom came back for one more thing, and you had the gun just like you do now," Billy explained.

Mr. Dodge squeezed his eyes closed and then opened them again. "I don't remember grabbing the gun," he said softly. "Is it loaded?"

"I don't know," Billy said.

Mr. Dodge loosened his grip on the gun. "Take it outside, Billy." He swallowed once and then continued in a weak voice. "Check it. Then bring it in. Empty." He released his grip on the gun and Billy grabbed it.

As Billy closed the door behind him Mr. Dodge turned to me and whispered, "You be careful on the river." He paused. "I'm going to make things right with Billy. I'm counting on you."

"I'll do my best," I said. Then I told Mr. Dodge what had happened the last couple of hours. He closed his eyes while I was talking but he nodded his head once or twice like he was listening. "I hope your head injury goes away," I finished.

Now he was breathing a little deeper, like maybe he'd fallen back asleep.

Billy walked back in. "It's empty now." He held up the gun with his good hand and then set it by the door. He put three shells on the windowsill. "Hopefully we won't need those. But we did just see a bear not too long ago. I'll reload it and walk you back once you make those knee pads."

I glanced at the gun. At least they had that. I swallowed the lump that had formed in my throat. Once I left, I wouldn't have anything to protect me from any animals.

# CHAPTER 41

**THE MOTHER** moose stood her ground. Her calf remained still with its ears standing straight up in an alert but nonthreatening way.

My socks were caked in mud, so every step I took I was like lifting at least five extra pounds. I liked it that the canoe was between me and the angry moose. If she did attack, I could use it as a barrier and back away. But if she stomped on the canoe and destroyed it, I'd be stuck walking in my socks through this burnt wasteland and maybe through an active fire.

I was drawing even with the mother moose now. She took a step toward me, her front legs now covered halfway in water.

I stopped.

Fifteen feet? Twenty feet? That's all that separated us. Out of the corner of my eye, I spied the smaller moose. It had turned and was facing me, too.

I was at the point where the next steps I took would put me as close, or closer to, the smaller moose than the mother.

Where is the perceived threat greatest?

How will the moose react?

When the wolves attacked the mother moose and her calf up the Olsen, the mother was constantly putting herself between the wolves and her calf, and then lashing out at them with her hooves. I had to expect the same.

If she destroyed the boat, I was in trouble.

But if she stomped on me, I'd be in more trouble.

Lining the canoe to this point had worked out, but I was now at the edge of the danger zone. At the edge of the make-the-wrong-move-and-get-yourself-killed zone.

I had to make a move. But not just any move. I had to make the right move for this particular time.

I was shivering from wearing wet clothes and sweating under my arms from fear and nervousness at the same time.

My feet had sunk to ankle depth in the mud. If I didn't move soon, I'd be stuck.

Okay, I thought. If I continue and get closer to the smaller moose, should I expect the mother to attack?

Yes.

How fast could she cross the deep water?

How far would I have to go beyond the smaller moose before the mother didn't see me as a threat?

*Go deep. Go deep.*

When I'd made the decision to line the canoe because I would be farther away from the moose than if I paddled, I was hoping the moose would leave me alone because of the water separating us. But now, I couldn't rule out the possibility that an angry moose would cross a slough to confront a perceived threat—to stomp me into oblivion. Especially if the slough was narrow and only the very middle was deep enough that it might have to swim for only a few feet.

*Deep is the key.*

"I hear you," I said softly. The deep water was my barrier, but was it enough?

*Stay deep.*

"How?"

"What do you mean?"

But my questions were met with silence.

I lifted one foot out of the mud to keep it from getting stuck, and the mother moose took another step deeper into the slough toward me. On one of her shoulders I noticed a long, jagged scar. What had she fought off successfully? A pack of wolves? A bear? A wolverine?

She'd done this before and had succeeded.

An experienced fighter.

Stay deep, my mind repeated.

I saw what I thought my father was suggesting I do. I wasn't sure if I was seeing exactly what he was trying to tell me, and I wasn't sure he was telling me the right thing. Then an image of Billy and his dad surrounded by flames flashed into my brain.

I had to give it try and hope I didn't die.

# CHAPTER 42

**CAREFULLY,** with as little movement as possible, I bent and leaned until I could grip the side of the canoe. I dropped the stern rope into the canoe and rested my hand on the rim. Then I dropped the bowline in and now grasped the canoe with both hands.

The mother moose remained in her about-to-charge position.

The next thing I did would probably make her charge. A thousand pounds of angry moose all focused on me.

With my knees already bent, I pushed off and hopped into the center of the canoe. I reached back, grabbed the paddle and saw splashes as she charged. I dug the tiny paddle into the water and pulled. I needed to stay in the center of the channel where the water was deepest.

I passed by the smaller moose but still heard splashes behind me. I glanced over my shoulder and saw hooves in the air. The mother moose was at the edge of the shallow water but had risen up like the moose I'd seen fending off the wolves.

I stuck my paddle in the water and pulled. I leaned forward, trying to distance myself from the hooves that were being directed toward me.

I was halfway through my next paddle stroke when the canoe jolted, like something had yanked it backwards or had come up from the bottom and rocked it violently. At the same time, I heard a loud knock, like wood smashing into wood. The entire front half of the canoe, including where I was sitting, rose up out of the water and then came down.

I let out a grunt as the bottom of the canoe slapped the surface and then I felt water pooling around my feet. I glanced back and saw the moose standing in chest high water, ears flat against her head. The back of the canoe had taken on some water, and where the rims of the canoe used to join at the stern, I now saw space and torn fabric. The ends of the rims were now separated by six or eight inches, and the fabric below them was torn, creating a space where water could splash in, or pour in if the canoe was riding low enough.

The moose must've connected with at least one hoof. And the water must've poured in when the canoe tipped up. But now that the weight of the moose was off the canoe, the newest hole in the canoe was riding just above the water.

I faced forward and paddled, stroke after stroke after stroke. At some point I'd stop and bail, but first I wanted to put more distance between me and the moose.

Stay deep, I thought as I paddled. The moose had gotten one good hit in. But if I had been in shallow water on either side of the slough, I would've been pummeled. I had to go toward her to get away from her. And then I thought of my uncle. Maybe I had to go toward him, too.

Options and choices.

Right now, my options were to go with him, if I survived this trip, or to run away. And somehow, I knew that running away wasn't the thing for me to do. I mean, where and how would I live? Especially in the winter in Alaska. No matter where I was, I wanted to live my life, not hide away.

So really, my only option was to go with him to Michigan. But, I realized, I had choices about *how* to go.

I could fight everything he does, or that I don't agree with, every step of the way.

I could totally cave in and just do whatever he says.

Or, I could choose something more in the middle.

Something that would allow him to see me for who I am. Something that would allow me to keep my identity and not get totally sucked into his world while at the same time respecting him for who he was. I didn't have to adopt his beliefs, but I could respect them as long as they were beliefs that were respectable.

Don't get me wrong. I didn't think any of this would all-of-a-sudden be easy. I mean, he was selling my house and kicking me out of my hometown, and planning on sending me to a religious school that I knew nothing about and expecting me to attend a church three times a week.

But maybe if I went with an open mind, it would make it more likely that he'd have one, too. Maybe he'd honor the way my parents raised me. And if he didn't, well, I'd have to deal with that. And no, I didn't have a solution if that happened except to be true to who I am. Of course, none of this would matter if I drowned or was burned up in a fire.

I sucked in a deep breath, and I became aware of the fabric from my underwear pressing against my mouth. Up ahead, I could see where the slough re-entered the main river.

The smoke was still pretty thick.

My eyes were aching.

I was hungry.

I was cold.

I'd almost gotten stomped by an angry moose.

I had another hole in my canoe.

But I was alive, and I was going to keep going until I found some help for my best friend and his dad.

# CHAPTER 43

## (BILLY AND HIS DAD)

"**THIS** first part is going to hurt," I said as I positioned the orange plastic sled on the floor next to my dad's bunk. From my bunk I grabbed my sleeping pad, sleeping bag and a pillow and put them in the sled. "This should help some."

"Okay, Billy." My dad forced himself up onto his elbows and started to slide himself over the side of the bunk. Now he had his hands on the floor, his good leg hanging off the bunk and his splinted leg still on the bunk. "I'm doing this for you. If I thought you didn't care, I'd flat out refuse. Now, grab my leg."

With my good arm, I scooped up his splinted leg, carried it over the side of the bunk, and set it down. He howled! But he was in the sled with his feet just hanging over the edge.

I stretched out the rope attached to the sled and tied it around my waist. Since I only had one good arm, I needed to use my body to pull him.

I glanced over my shoulder and said, "Brace yourself." I leaned into the rope and my legs tightened up. The sled slid about a foot. My dad was heavy.

"I can help with arms," my dad said. "On the count of three, you pull."

I looked back again and saw him with his palms on the floor.

On three I pulled, and the sled jerked forward and started sliding. We made it out the door and onto the porch into the thick yellow smoke and were now facing the steps which I had covered with a narrow piece of plywood, making a ramp. The air was hot and heavy—a thick, yellow, sulfur stew—and the red glow seemed to be everywhere.

My dad coughed and then grabbed his head. I could tell he was in pain. I just hoped his head injury wasn't so serious that all this movement would kill him, but I didn't have a choice if I wanted to try to save him.

"Pull me to the edge of the ramp, and then untie. "I'll muscle myself down the ramp, otherwise I might run you over."

I did as he said and at the bottom of the ramp, I retied the rope and started pulling him toward the river. The hot wind was trying to blow me sideways, but I kept driving forward.

When we reached the edge of the water I stopped and turned around and I could see flames in the trees behind the cabin.

"It's coming fast," I said. "We need to get into the water."

My dad was slumped over in the sled like he'd just run a marathon at full speed.

"I'm going to pull you into the water," I explained, as I stepped into the shallows. Once I got the sled partway in, I guided it with my good hand until my dad was covered in water with just his head sticking out. "We might have to go deeper, depending on the flames."

Trees were flaming on both sides of the cabin now and I knew it was just a matter of minutes before it caught and burned. I had some other things on the porch I'd planned on having with us but it was too late to go back for them now. I hoped the air wouldn't get so hot that we'd be baked and boiled right where we sat.

"You did it," my dad whispered. "If we die, we won't die alone." He reached out a put a hand on my shoulder.

"No matter what happens," I said, "we're in this together."

# CHAPTER 44

**I KEPT** paddling from the middle of the boat, trying to keep my weight as far away from both holes as possible. The main river was moving like a high-speed train compared to the sluggish slough I'd been in. The headwind had turned into a cross breeze, so I paddled mostly on the right side to keep the canoe from getting blown around.

I set my paddle down, reached behind me and grabbed my kneepads, then put them under my knees, which were aching from pressing down on the knobby wood frame of the canoe floor.

The hole in the back of the canoe wasn't taking on much water at the moment since it was riding above the waterline. If the river got wavy, that would change. The red fanny pack covering the hole in the front of the canoe was still letting some water in. I leaned forward and pressed down onto the fanny pack. Then I picked up the pot and started bailing because I didn't know where the point of no return was. If the river got wavy and water started pouring into the hole in the stern, this boat could sink fast.

I bailed until there was an inch or two of water sloshing around in the canoe then I kept on paddling.

My shoulders and back ached from using the tiny nub of a paddle.

Up ahead, I could see a big expanse of sand. Like a large flat island with no vegetation. But something was different about it compared to other islands I'd seen.

A valley. Another river valley was opening to the left.

And on the far side of the valley, I saw something I hadn't seen for miles and miles. A dark green haze blanketing the shore.

Spruce trees, I realized. Unburnt spruce trees. The smoke was still a thick yellow toxic stew that stung my eyes, but it looked like the fire itself had been stopped by the big tributary coming into the Tanana.

I was paddling next to the sandy island now and was able to see up the tributary a ways. It was a broad expanse of sand and gravel bars with no vegetation on them. Compared to the Tanana there wasn't much water flowing, but the valley itself was wide, like maybe at some point in the past there had been a lot of water.

Maybe without trees on the islands, the fire hadn't been able to jump the big river valley. Blackened shore on one side faced off with green on the other.

The water was the same silty gray brown of the Tanana, so I knew that somewhere beyond where I could see—somewhere through the yellow haze that engulfed everything—there were glaciers feeding this river too.

Now I was paddling next to a shore with green spruce trees. I'd kept to the left side of the river. Across the river, on the right bank, I could make out the mostly burnt spruce forest, with tiny patches of birch that had been spared.

Blisters were forming on my hands from gripping the tiny paddle, but I kept on digging the blade through the water, thankful for the current and the lack of a headwind. Water was still coming into the canoe at a steady pace, and I was dreading having to bail again but knew I'd have to soon.

Up ahead, the river was taking a sharp bend to the right. A gravel bar in the distance stretched out from the left riverbank. On the gravel bar, I saw little bumps.

Red bumps.

Yellow bumps.

Blue bumps.

Some of the bumps were moving.

People.

As I got closer to the gravel bar, people were gathering and pointing in my direction.

Maybe they could just tell that I needed some help because when I got close to shore, two men and a woman waded into the river, grabbed the canoe and pulled it in.

I set my paddle down and stood up. My knees were so tight from all the kneeling that they buckled, and two people grabbed me before I fell.

"I'm okay," I tried to say but my voice was barely working. I stepped out of the canoe and stood, and the people let go of me after a moment.

I took in the faces. Now there were at least thirty of them staring at me.

A man with a short beard, holding a red helmet in his hands said, "What happened?"

I shivered once. Then I coughed. "I," I started, and then coughed again. A shiver ran through my body.

"Bring some hot soup, and some dry clothes," the man yelled over his shoulder before I could respond. Then he turned back to me. "You're wearing underwear over your face."

I nodded and then pulled the underwear over my head. "Smoke was pretty thick," I said, finding my voice. "I lost all my gear."

He nodded. "Go on."

"My friends," I said. "They're about fifty miles up the Olsen. They're hurt. They need help. They need to get out of there. I thought I'd have to go all the way to the bridge."

The man turned to the woman standing next to him. "Radio for a chopper. Get it in the air and up the Olsen. We've got to get those people out of there now." Then he turned back to me. "Fifty miles up the Olsen is a long way from here. You've already come over one hundred river miles, easily. The bridge is about another hundred downriver. We were flown to this spot to fight the fire. Otherwise, there'd be no one here." The man glanced at the canoe. "You paddled in that?" He reached in the canoe and pulled out what was left of my paddle. "With this? All the way here?" He shook his head. Then he put his hand on the splinted rim of the canoe. "Did this gunwale break during your trip?"

I nodded. "A burnt-up tree fell on it."

A few people were pulling their phones out, taking pictures or videos, but I didn't care.

Then I felt my body starting to sway. Two people caught me as I was falling and gently sat me on the ground. My eyes started to close but I forced them open.

I said, "I followed the river."

# CHAPTER 45

## [EPILOGUE]

**FOUR** and a half days had elapsed from the time I left the cabin to the time I met up with the firefighters where the Johnson River flows into the Tanana, and during that time I'd paddled about one hundred miles and gotten about four hours of sleep. I don't think I conquered my fears by paddling that old canoe. What I think is that some amount of fear can be good if it doesn't paralyze you. If it doesn't make you freeze up and do nothing. If I learned anything on the river it was that recognizing my fear, instead of putting energy into fighting it, helped me to keep doing difficult things when I was scared out of my mind.

The Fire Service camp I paddled to on the river got a helicopter in the air and rescued Billy and Mr. Dodge. Mr. Dodge was fading in and out of consciousness when they got him to a hospital. He's going to make it. Billy's mom is divorcing him, and Billy is moving to Seattle to live with his mother.

And me, right now I'm on a jet that's about to take off—bound for Michigan.

Even though I was still scared and nervous about going to Michigan and was still majorly bummed about my uncle selling the house and land, I needed to give him a chance to be the person stepping in after both my parents died. He was choosing to do that.

I still didn't know how I was going to deal with the new religious school and him expecting me to go to church three times a week. Somewhere in my life there had to be some space to be myself and to stay connected to my mom and dad.

*You are in charge of your own beliefs. No one can take that away from you.*

Somehow, I'd try to respect my uncle's beliefs while not letting go of my own. I just hoped we had some common ground to stand on.

A few minutes after take-off, out of the window of the jet I could see the Tanana River below me. In my mind I was already working on ways to get back to Alaska, back to my home.

And at the same time, no matter how much I wished that I didn't have to leave, no matter how much I couldn't wait to return to Alaska, I've still got my life to live.

And the time to live it is now.

# ALSO BY PAUL GRECI

*Surviving Bear Island*

*The Wild Lands*

*Hostile Territory*

Photo by Ben Lazar

**PꓘUL GREꓵi** has lived and worked in Alaska for over 30 years as a teacher, field biology technician in remote wilderness areas, and a backpacking trip leader for teens. He loves exploring the wilderness by foot, kayak, canoe, and snowshoe. His middle grade adventure novel, *Surviving Bear Island*, was a Junior Library Guild Selection and a Scholastic Reading Club Pick. He is also the author of the young adult novels *Hostile Territory* and *The Wild Lands*.